The One That Got Away

PRIYANKA MENON discovered the wonderful world of romance after her standard X exams, when her aunt secretly gifted her two Mills & Boon novels. That summer was the beginning of her journey and torrid affair with romance novels. On the one hand, she can effortlessly quote Jane Austen and Thomas Hardy, and on the other, Penny Jordan, Diana Palmer, Jane Potter, and many more romance authors she has grown up reading.

Priyanka is a Spoken-Word poet and an integral part of the Spoken-Word poetry circle in Pune, where she lives. She is also a lecturer in advertising and English literature. For leisure, she loves watching reruns of *The Wonder Years*, reading comic books, and dissing saas-bahu soap operas with her grandmother. She believes that she gets her writing powers from red-velvet pastries and white-chocolate mochas at Starbucks.

You can write to her at priyankamenon.author@gmail.com

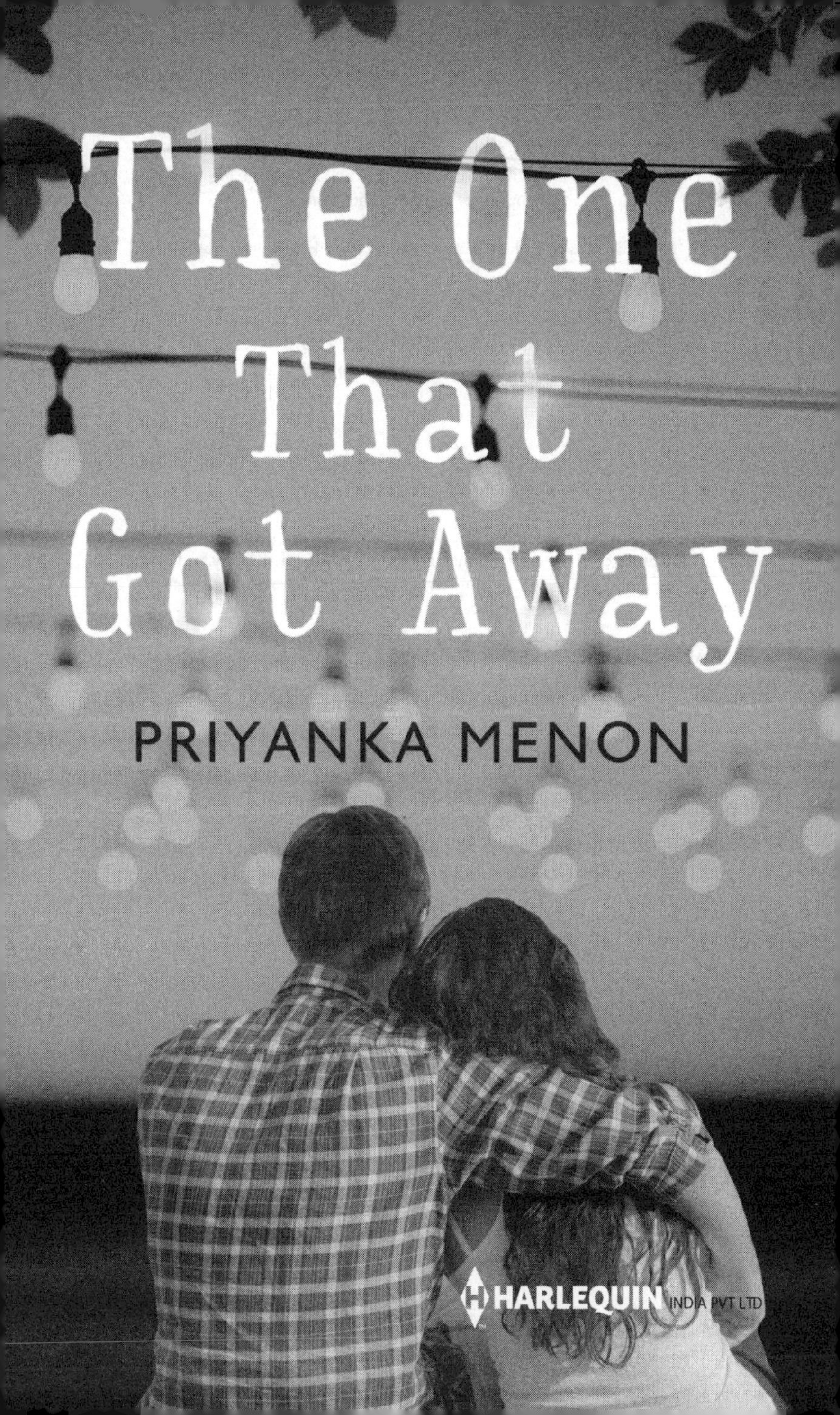
The One That Got Away
PRIYANKA MENON
HARLEQUIN INDIA PVT LTD

First published in India in 2015 by Harlequin
An imprint of HarperCollins *Publishers*

This edition is published by arrangement with Harlequin Books S.A.

P-ISBN: 978-93-5106-797-9
E-ISBN: 978-93-5106-801-3

2 4 6 8 10 9 7 5 3 1

HarperCollins *Publishers*
A-75, Sector 57, Noida, Uttar Pradesh 201301, India
1 London Bridge Street, London, SE1 9GF, United Kingdom
Hazelton Lanes, 55 Avenue Road, Suite 2900, Toronto, Ontario M5R 3L2
and 1995 Markham Road, Scarborough, Ontario M1B 5M8, Canada
25 Ryde Road, Pymble, Sydney, NSW 2073, Australia
195 Broadway, New York, NY 10007, USA

Typeset in 11.5/15 Bembo Regular at
Manipal Digital Systems, Manipal

Printed and bound at
Thomson Press (India) Ltd

For Hrishav, my knight on an orange tricycle

Prologue

The train was leaving the platform. Shyamita sat on the edge of her seat, looking out of the window, trying to catch a glimpse of her best friend. School was over. They would now have to go their separate ways. And yet, somehow, she couldn't bring herself to bid goodbye to those precious moments she had shared with Jai.

She was going to pursue a career in dance at Kalaniketan Bharanatyam Dance Institute under the tutelage of Guru Meenakshi Amma. Jai would be going to Cardiff for his undergrad studies. It had been his dream ever since she had met him and she knew how hard he had worked to get that scholarship. She had gone along with him to all those British Council scholarship seminars and application sessions.

But what if they never met again? What if this was where they were meant to say goodbye? Their board exam results would be sent home. So they didn't have any reason to come back to school.

They had to be adults now. And being an adult meant that they would probably never see each other again. Shyamita's heart broke into tiny pieces as this thought sank in.

Jai had pulled the chain.

The blaring horn of the train signalling its final departure broke her reverie. Where was Jai? Was he not even coming to say goodbye? She wanted to meet her best friend one last time. She had so much to tell him. She wanted to tell him everything – how she felt about him, *how she'd always felt about him*...and she wanted to hear him say the same things. Two months ago, on Valentine's Day, she had picked out a beautiful Archies' card from the store near school. The words in the card were just what she had always wanted to say to him. But she had never gotten around to giving it to him. *Perhaps, today*...

The train had gained a little speed, when it suddenly jerked. The screeching of the wheels against the tracks caused a terrible sound in the otherwise noiseless first-class compartment. Shyamita looked out of the window to find railway guards running beside the tracks. What was going on?

Suddenly, the door to the bogey was wrenched open. Shyamita looked up to find Jai, slightly breathless, standing in the doorway, with two small ice-cream cups in his hand. On either side of him were the two railway guards she had seen a few minutes ago.

1

Mumbai was as crowded as ever. Nothing seemed to have changed. Twelve years ago, Shyamita had bid goodbye to this city. And now she was back. She was quite content with what she had accomplished. She was now a successful artist, living in Paris. Her work was celebrated in galleries across Europe, and soon she was going to open her own gallery in Singapore. She had made something of herself. *Despite the accident.*

The taxi-driver regaled her with stories of how Mumbai was an ever-changing city. Every day he would drive close to seventy-five people from one part of the city to another. Shyamita tried to drown out his voice and focused on what she would have to do in the coming days. Geet Chadda was marrying the man of her dreams. She had endured hours of Geet rambling on about how Karan was her soulmate and how happy they were.

Geet and Karan were high-school sweethearts.

Shyamita hated that phrase! She hated it as much as she hated the other phrase that people all across the world swore by. *Love at first sight.*

'I mean, seriously?' Shyamita had asked Mia, her flatmate in Paris. 'How can you fall in love with someone at first sight?'

Mia had smiled softly and told her that she would know one day. Shyamita had brushed off her comment as coming from someone who was ruled by pregnancy hormones. Mia was almost nine months pregnant. The father of her baby was her boyfriend of fifteen years. When Shyamita had asked her why she didn't want to live with Michael, Mia told her that they were *not ready*.

Another term Shyamita did not get. Her brother, Shaunak constantly teased her by saying that she shouldn't be living in Paris. According to him, his sister should live in a village in a mud hut.

But Shaunak didn't get it either. Nobody did. Nobody knew that Shyamita had fallen in love once, irrevocably.

It was a secret that she kept to herself.

Jairam Nair. Just his name was enough to set Shyamita's heart aflutter. He had been her best friend when they were in school. They had been inseparable – joined at the hip, some of their teachers would tease them. Thinking about those times made Shyamita smile. Even after so many years, she still remembered each and every moment she had spent with Jai. Some of the best years of her life were spent in school along with her best friends, Jai, Geet, and Karan.

She and Jai had been boarders. Geet and Karan were day-scholars and lived with their parents. Shyamita's father had been an officer in the Indian Army, and was therefore posted to some of the most remote places in the country. During her early years, she had also traveled with her parents. But when she was promoted to standard eight, her parents had made a conscious decision to not have her hop schools and so she stayed in Mumbai, not moving when her father was transferred.

She closed her eyes to drain out the noise of the city as well as the chit-chat the taxi-driver insisted on maintaining. The last time she had met Jai had been nearly twelve years ago, on the last day of school, at the railway station.

She had to go to Kolkata for her cousin's wedding. She was going by train to Delhi and from there, her brother Shaunak would fly with her to Kolkata. Jai had spent the previous night in Shyamita's hostel room, climbing in through the window after the warden had slept. They had spent the night huddled together over a bunch of history notes and previous years' question papers, preparing for their last exam. Every now and then, Jai would crack a joke about their history teacher and Shyamita would start cackling so hard that she would have tears streaming down her cheeks. Jai would always say that she was the only girl he knew who could laugh like nobody was watching. 'You even snort, Mithi,' he'd say, and a pillow would be flung in his direction.

But the next day, after the paper, as Shyamita bid goodbye to all her friends and teachers, Jai was nowhere to be seen. She hated to think that he was celebrating the end of the exams with Aisha, his latest girlfriend. She despised the girl.

She waited for him for as long as she could. But finally, she had to leave for the railway station. She stuffed her luggage into the boot of the taxi and climbed into the backseat of the old Fiat. Clutching her backpack, which had the card she had picked up for Jai two months ago, she told the driver to take her to the station. In the front passenger seat sat Sunil kaka, the school's attendant. The matron had asked him to drop Shyamita to the station, make sure she was comfortably seated and then return. The old man struck up a conversation with the taxi driver. Angrily dashing the tears that were forming in her eyes, Shyamita cursed Aisha, then Jai, and then Aisha again.

Upon reaching the station, she frantically scanned the crowds for any sign of Jai, but she couldn't see him. She got into the first-class compartment and stowed her luggage under her seat. Then sat down and waited, willing her best friend to make a final appearance and at least say goodbye. But none of that happened. As the train left the station, Shyamita was beyond upset. She thought she would give Jai the card she had picked up from Archies' and finally tell him how she felt. She felt betrayed.

The train suddenly jerked to a screeching halt. Shyamita peered out of her window to see two constables running down the tracks, when the door to her bogey was wrenched open.

Jai stood there, still wearing his school uniform and bearing two ice-cream cups in his hand and said, with a hint of anger, 'Thought you'll leave without saying goodbye to me, Mithi?'

He was angry? How dare he? Shyamita thought. 'You were supposed to come with me to the station, Jai. Where were you?' she inquired in an angry hiss.

'I was in the staff room,' he replied. Shyamita was perplexed. 'What were you doing in there?'

'That's between Ms Jacinta and me,' was his bristling response.

But Shyamita was still angry. 'Where is Aisha?' she asked, bitingly.

'Who?' It was Jai's turn to look confused now.

'Aisha...your girlfriend, where is she?'

Jai took a moment to reply. Taking a deep breath he said, 'You really think Aisha is my girlfriend, Mithi?'

'Yes.'

'Here we go, madamjee,' the taxi-driver announced that they had arrived at Geet's house. Shyamita sat up with a jerk and realized that she had fallen asleep on the way. Annoyed with the driver for not letting her sleep a little longer, and at the same time relieved that she wouldn't have to relive the climax of her dream again, she got out of the car, paid him the fare, and hauled her bags to the porch.

'Shyamuuuuuuuu...!'

Here we go, she thought.

Geet came screaming to the front verandah and enveloped Shyamita in a bone-crushing hug. Shyamita hugged her right back. Though she was very happy for her friend, Shyamita felt a small pang of envy for the girl who had everything going for her.

Geet was a typical Indian bride. She was fair, with beautiful almond shaped eyes, long black hair that fell way past her waist and the perfect hourglass figure. She was a jewelry designer and had showrooms all over India. Shyamita was very happy for her friend, she really was. But there were times when she wished she could have switched places with Geet, just so that she could be with her high school love.

But Shyamita knew she was nothing like Geet. Her complexion was dusky and she had light brown eyes that were too big for her face. Her hair was brown and curly and her figure, which had once been like an hourglass, was not quite the same now. She called herself chubby. And at just five feet two inches, that wasn't a good thing at all.

The wedding house was a sight to behold. Decked with flowers and streaming lights, there was music and dance flowing from every room in the house. Shyamita was ushered to her room by Geet's mother, Neetu Aunty, who chattered all the way. She went on and on about how blessed her daughter was to have found the man of her dreams, and how Karan was such a wonderful son already. Apparently he never made her feel like she was his mother-in-law. He had always seen her as his mother.

Shyamita was given her old room in Geet's house. It was an extension to Geet's room that her father had installed, so that the two girls could sleep comfortably when Shyamita used to come for sleepovers. In her opinion, Geet's father had gone a little overboard; when all he really needed to do was to put another bed in Geet's room. But Deepak Uncle had been known for his extravagance.

Mumbai was always hot and humid. And today was no exception. But Shyamita liked the hot and sticky weather. It reminded her of another time. A time when she and Jai would go to Chowpatty from their hostels and have delicious local specialties – like pani puri. After eating about seventy pani puris (that was their combined best) they would walk down to the beach and let the sand and waves take over the next hour of their lives. Shyamita could never recall a time she was happier than she was then. Even the many delights of Paris, Amsterdam, Madrid, New York, Buenos Aires and several other cities she had visited over the years, paled in comparison to the pleasure and happiness she had felt in doing the simplest of things in Mumbai. But deep down, she knew why the rest of the places had never held any appeal for her. Jai wasn't there.

And that was her problem even today. She hadn't seen him till now. She knew he would come for Geet's wedding; she had been mentally preparing herself to meet him. But she was annoyed that he wasn't there to receive her when she had arrived at Geet's house. She wondered if he was still upset about the last time they had met. But more than anything, she just wanted to see her best friend. It had been too long.

Where the hell are you, Jai?

Linking Road was as crowded as ever. There were swarms of people crowding each and every tiny store. About fifty people were crammed into shops that were probably no bigger than a minivan. Street children were scampering up and down on either side of the road. Beggars were begging for alms, car horns were blaring, buses were heaving… and Jairam Nair, bestselling author and closet-poet was waiting for his best friend, Karan Walia, to hurry up with his shopping. In his mind, Jai had already penned a few couplets in praise of his friend's time-management qualities. Karan's last-minute shopping was for his honeymoon – two pairs of shorts, and a few pairs of beachwear slippers. Karan was the only son of one of the country's richest industrialists and of Mumbai's most respected citizens. But clearly that didn't deter him from shopping for his honeymoon on Linking Road.

Jairam, or Jai as he was known to his loved ones, was most definitely annoyed. He knew for a fact that Karan was nowhere close to being done with his shopping. Based on his friend's track record, Jai was sure that Karan would easily take another hour to get done. But this, Jai would not allow. He needed to go to Geet's house. There was somebody there who he had to meet.

Shyamita Bose. Just her name was enough to bring a smile to his lips. All throughout school they had been the best of friends. Even their teachers had called them inseparable. The two of them had had the best of times. *And the worst of times too*, a voice inside his head reminded him.

Mumbai had been good to him, he had to admit. Seven years ago, he'd returned from London, where he'd completed his masters in English, with a side-major in Creative Writing. And the city had welcomed him with open arms once again. The initial days hadn't been easy. Sharing apartments with untidy and temperamental people, not to mention rodents, cockroaches and other forms of arachnoids had most definitely not been easy. But the success of his first book turned his world around. Literary agents and publishers had flocked to him, and within no time at all, he'd written two more bestsellers. Today, he had five bestsellers under his name, his latest one having made it to the *New York Times* Bestsellers list, and a trilogy that he was working on. In all this, the one thing that had remained constant was his love for Mumbai. It had given him everything. He'd built a new life here. And he was damned proud of that life.

After another half an hour of silent mutiny, Jai was finally rewarded. Karan was miraculously done with his shopping and was now ready to go back to the hotel where his cousins and extended family were staying. Karan's parents had their own house in Mumbai, but he was staying at the hotel to spend more time with his cousins who had come for the wedding from different parts of the world.

Jai dropped Karan back at the hotel and was on his way to Geet's house when his mobile phone rang. It was his sister calling to remind him that she and their mother would be arriving by the evening flight. God-damn-it! This meant he had just less than three hours before he had to be at the airport. Geet's house was about thirty minutes from the hotel, but the traffic in Mumbai was another story.

As he drove to Geet's, Jai recalled the number of times he and Shyamita would hop onto a bus during the weekends and go to Marine Drive. There they would binge on some chaat and cutting chai before Shyamita dragged him to the beach saying he had had enough to eat. Over the past twelve years, not a single day had gone by when he hadn't thought of his best friend. Life had changed immediately after school. Priorities had shifted.

He could never erase their last meeting from his memory. He had behaved badly. He knew he had. But he had been pushed. He had not known how to react to certain questions Shyamita had asked. And for him, up until that moment, he had always considered Shyamita as someone he could talk to about anything without worrying about how she would take it. She would give him her honest opinion, always.

But on that day, just after the paper, Jai's world had tilted off its already precarious axis. He had been called into the staff room by Ms Jacinta, their English teacher. She sat him down and told him how proud she was about how he far he had come along. Jai had not had the best of childhoods and his first few months in his new school had not been very good either. He had had difficulties in adjusting to the people around him and his insecurities had been too many. It was Ms Jacinta who had helped him cope with all the added pressures and in adjusting to his new life as a boarder. She had always been his favorite teacher.

'How was your paper, Jai?' she inquired kindly after he sat down.

'It wasn't too bad, madam. I can't expect it to be any better than it was. History is not really my strong suit,' he replied with a smile.

'Yours and Shyamita's, I'm sure,' Ms Jacinta added.

'Yes, Mithi's too,' he said.

'I like that name you have for her,' she said with a smile. 'I'm glad you two are such good friends.'

'Yes, we are. Thank you, madam,' Jai said. 'In fact, I must be off soon. Mithi has to leave for the railway station in a while. I need to go with her.'

'Is she just your friend, Jai?' Ms Jacinta fired another question.

Jai took a moment to reply. He just stared blankly at his English teacher. He found it awkward that she chose to ask him something so personal.

'Umm...yes, madam. She's just a friend,' he said finally, fidgeting in his chair.

After a pause which felt like an eternity to Jai, Ms Jacinta said, 'Okay. But I want you to promise me one thing, Jai.' She was teary-eyed now.

'I want you to make something good of yourself. You are a wonderful young man with great potential. Do not waste your time worrying about the past. All the wrongs in the world have a way of correcting themselves. That's how things work. So do not bust your head over it. Okay?'

Jai looked at his teacher with a mixture of respect and gratitude. 'Yes, madam. I promise.'

'You and Shyamita are two of my favorite students. I know I'm not supposed to have favorites,' she added hastily when she saw Jai's eyes widen. 'I hope the two of you will always be good friends and not let time and distance come in the way. I have seen this happen to too many of my students,' she added, her tears flowing freely now.

Jai stood up and went over to her desk and gave her a hug. He was really going to miss this kind-hearted woman. But as he bid her goodbye and walked out of the staffroom, he thought about what she had said about him and Shyamita. He didn't know what he was supposed to make of it.

He glanced at his watch and realized he was really late. Mithi would have already left for the railway station, but not before cursing him, he was sure. He smiled as he recalled the number of times she would curse him in one day. His Mithi was one raging spitfire.

❧❧

One hour and fifteen minutes later, Jai was at Geet's doorstep. He would have to leave for the airport in about forty minutes.

Would that be enough time to mend bridges?

2

The hot shower felt absolutely divine. Despite the heat and humidity outside, Shyamita had always preferred her bath water to be hot. She stepped out of the bathroom in a white robe with lavender flowers on it. Her curls were wrapped in a towel, turban-style. She was standing in front of her open suitcase, contemplating on what to wear, when there was a knock on her door.

'Who is it?'

'Shyamu, open the door,' came Geet's voice.

Shyamita didn't think twice, went to the door and wrenched it open. *Big mistake.*

Geet stood there, that evil little thing, grinning from ear to ear, and right behind her was Jai – wearing a pair of white linen pants, a blue polo t-shirt and wicker moccasins. He slid his Ray Ban aviators into the pocket of his t-shirt. You could always count on him to make a surprising entry.

Shyamita stood frozen. Twelve years had passed since the last time she had seen her best friend. Twelve years on, and Jai still looked the same. Granted he had started to grey near his temples, but the man looked absolutely stunning. Six feet tall, wavy dark black hair that curled into the collar of his polo neck, dark brown eyes, and a smile that could disarm an entire platoon, Jai had always been… well, sexy! But this time around there was something else that caught Shyamita's attention. It wasn't his smile, not even his eyes. It was the light stubble that was grazing his jaw-line and chin. He looked more rakish now. The boyhood innocence had been replaced by a rugged masculinity. Her heart skipped a couple of beats.

Shyamita didn't realize that she was standing stock-still until Geet cleared her throat loudly, 'Ahem! I'm going to leave you to continue to stare at each other while I go and get ready for the engagement. Buh-bye!' She turned and left.

Now it was just the two of them. Shyamita was still not able to say anything. But she made a mental note to kill Geet later.

'Hi, Mithi,' Jai used the nickname he had given her.

'Hi,' she whispered in reply.

'Can I come in?'

'Umm…yeah, sure,' the uncertainty in her heart echoed in her voice. She stepped aside to let him enter.

'Er…Mithi, you might want to put some clothes on…,' Jai muttered.

Shyamita was immediately pulled out of her reverie. She wasn't even wearing any underwear for god's sake!

'Er… yeah, okay,' she shut the door in Jai's face.

Oh shit! I am such an idiot. Shyamita cursed herself as she rummaged through her suitcase to find something appropriate to wear. She quickly pulled on a grey top with yellow and pink flowers. She was about to pull on a pair of jeans, when she realized she still hadn't worn any underwear. She got dressed, quickly removed the towel from her hair, and was running her fingers through her tangled curly hair even as she opened the door.

Jai wasn't prepared for the onslaught of emotions that swept through him when he first laid eyes on Shyamita. Twelve years had passed since the last time he had seen her. They'd gone from being best friends to strangers. Not only had they not kept in touch, but neither had even tried to reach out to the other at any point. It was as though both had wanted to forget each other. *Like that would ever happen*, he mentally snorted.

In a white and lavender robe with a towel wrapped around her head, Shyamita looked nothing like his best friend. In her place was this voluptuous and beautiful goddess, with big almond-shaped eyes, thick long lashes and a pink, lush mouth, who had managed to render him speechless for close to five minutes. The slight parting of the lapels of her robe presented him with a small but tantalizing glimpse of her cleavage. Jai was stunned that his brain was entertaining such thoughts about the girl with whom he used to talk about other girls. Back in school, Shyamita was just one of the boys. He could talk about anything and everything with her; and that was perhaps why *she* had been his best friend and not any other boy.

It was Geet's snarky comment about them staring at each other while she prepared for other ceremonies that finally got him to open his mouth. And then, like a complete idiot, he had made Shyamita feel all awkward and had deservedly had the door slammed in his face.

He waited for a solemn seven minutes, before he decided to knock on her door. Just as he raised his fist, the door opened and there she stood. His Mithi. Her feet were bare and he could see her toenails had been painted a bright pink. She was running her fingers through her tangled hair. Jai's breath hitched. How on earth was he going to have a rational conversation with this woman without making an utter fool of himself, he knew not. He was shocked by this trail of thought. Previously, it had been so easy to talk to her. From problems in mathematics to pushing her to go and talk to a girl he liked, he had been able to tell her just about everything.

But today he was hesitating. Why? Was it because she had changed? Or was it because he had? Or perhaps, was it because neither had changed, but were too afraid to admit it?

Was she still his Mithi?

'Hi,' she quipped, slightly breathless. Shyamita was sure her face resembled a beetroot, or else a tomato. She had never felt more shy or awkward in her life. And this was Jai for god's sake. This was her best friend from school. Why was there any kind of awkwardness?

'Hi, Mithi. How have you been?'

'I am well, Jai. Why don't you come in?' She said a little too formally. She stepped aside, allowing him to enter her room.

'Thanks.' He strolled in with his hands in his pockets. He stopped in the middle of the room, turned around and simply stared at her.

Okay, now I'm definitely a beetroot!

There was a rosewood lovers' seat at the foot of the huge four-poster bed. She motioned for him to sit down there.

'Ladies first,' he said and smiled softly.

Shyamita knew why. She had always hated that phrase when they were in school. She had never been able to understand the need to say something like that. According to her, it didn't uphold the principles of gender equality. She had always believed that by saying 'ladies first', the person who was saying it was in fact making it obvious that he believed that the lady was weaker and therefore needed special care.

Shyamita smiled now and said, 'Just sit down, Jai.'

He sat down and motioned for her to sit next to him.

Uh-oh! Awkward scene coming up.

Shyamita's heart was beating so fast and hard that she was sure Jai could hear it. She shook her head and said, 'No thanks. I have some unpacking to do. Would you mind if I did that now?'

Jai looked at her, perplexed. 'Er…yeah, sure. Go ahead.'

She started with the small suitcase and the travel bag. She lifted them off the table that sat right next to the dresser and put them onto the bed. She knew that she was stretching the silence but for the life of her, she didn't know what to say. She needed to figure out a way to strike up a conversation with her best friend, whom she hadn't seen in nearly twelve years.

Were they still best friends?

Jai watched Shyamita as she moved about the room. She had always been graceful in her movements. He knew dance had always been her greatest passion and yet he had never gone to see her perform, except for that one disastrous time. He was proud of all her accomplishments. He felt like they were his own. But he just wouldn't go to any of her performances. She had even asked him once about his weird behavior and that was when they had had a huge row.

'Why don't you ever come to my performances?' she had innocently asked one evening. They had just finished celebrating her winning an award for her dance and had been sitting in the school hall doing their week's homework. Given that they were in the ninth grade, their teachers had piled them with homework and extra assignments, already preparing them for the next academic year. Tenth grade meant board exams and the teachers were anxious about the whole deal.

'I just don't understand all that, Mithi,' he had replied, with as much nonchalance as he could muster.

'What is it that you don't understand, Jai?'

'I just don't...'

'The fact is you're not interested. You really don't care about any of these things,' Shyamita had said and stalked off to her hostel block before he could say anything in his defense. Jai knew he had really hurt her. But he didn't know what to say to her. So he thought it best to keep quiet and wait for her to come back and talk to him. *Big mistake!* Not only did Shyamita not talk to him for a fortnight, she also went to Goa with Geet without telling him.

Then one night, close to midnight, the warden of his dormitory woke him up saying there was a call for him. Groggily, cursing whoever it was that was calling him at such an ungodly hour, Jai went to answer the phone call.

The next three minutes were the worst of his life. A frantic Geet told him that Shyamita had almost drowned at Candolim beach. She had been rescued by a couple of boys and was admitted to the local hospital. But she hadn't regained consciousness.

For the next few hours Jai operated on autopilot. He rushed back to his dormitory, pulled out a bag from under his bed and stuffed some clothes into it. He then removed his pillow from its case, and took out a wad of notes. He had been saving up for a trip to Delhi for a literary fest. But right then, he needed to get to Shyamita. Nothing else mattered.

On his way out, he quickly scribbled a note to the hostel warden who had promptly gone back to sleep after waking him up, saying there had been an emergency and that he would be back in a couple of days. He knew he was going to be in major trouble when he returned, but he would worry about that later. For most of his life Jai had learnt to fend for himself. His mother had taught him that. Most children his age would have found it difficult to make decisions let alone follow through with them. But Jai was different, which was why in less than an hour he was on his way to Goa in a bus.

By ten o'clock the next morning, Jai was in the hospital room where Shyamita had been admitted. His heart sank. She looked so small and fragile. Never before had he felt so helpless. He couldn't do anything to make her better. So instead, he started talking to her. He told her about how sorry he was for not having been a good friend. He told her about how much he had missed her during the last couple of weeks. And finally, he also told her about why he wouldn't come to any of her performances.

'The truth is Mithi,' he began softly, 'I do not like the idea of you dancing in front of so many people. I know how much you love your dance, but I cannot watch you dancing to an audience. And it isn't because I am old-fashioned or anything of that sort. No Mithi, I am just selfish. I want you to dance only for me.'

To this day, Jai didn't know whether Shyamita had actually heard him that morning in Goa. By that afternoon she regained consciousness. The doctors had kept her under observation for one more night, and Jai had insisted on sleeping in the same room on the makeshift bed. The two of them had agreed that it would be pointless to inform her parents as she was much better now. The journey back to Mumbai was spent in awkward silence, with only Geet muttering every half an hour or so that she was never going to go with Shyamita to a beach again.

As Jai watched Shyamita now, he realized just how much he had missed her this last decade. He had already moved to Cardiff when he had heard about her accident from Karan. He'd felt just as helpless then. He'd wanted to call her and find out if she was alright. But for some reason, he couldn't bring himself to do it. Over the years, through Karan, he'd learnt that she had studied art in Jaisalmer, Kolkata, and even in Tanjore before moving to Paris to pursue her masters. He was proud of the life she had carved out for herself. She had always been a terrific artist and somewhere deep down he had had this niggling doubt that perhaps she was being pushed into dance by her parents. He wanted to know about her accident, but he didn't know how to broach the subject.

But for now, he had to go. He didn't want to make his mother and sister wait at the airport. He'd get an earful from both of them.

Getting to his feet, he said, 'Umm…Mithi, I need to leave now. I've to go pick up Amma and Naina from the airport.'

'Oh wow! Naina's coming? How is she?' she asked him excitedly and, for the first time, addressed him directly.

'Yes, she and Amma are coming. Naina likes to drive me up the wall every now and then,' he smiled.

'That is fantastic. I haven't seen her in ages. I think the last time I saw her was when she and Lalita Aunty had come to Mumbai for your sixteenth birthday,' she said. 'Do you remember? We'd gone to Leopold's.'

'I know. We can all catch up. Anyway, I've got to go now. Otherwise, the two of them will collectively pull out all my hair. See you really soon.'

'Say hi to Lalita Aunty and Naina,' she said.

He nodded, a dazzling smile crinkling the corners of his eyes. 'Yes, Mithi.'

3

'So did you tell her?' Naina asked Jai.

'Tell her what?' he quipped.

'Do not get cute with me, Jairam Nair,' his little sister retorted.

'Hey! You've just landed. Can you cut out the interrogation and give your brother a hug?'

'Sure. But right after you tell me what you said to Shyamita,' she insisted.

Jai looked to his mother for some support, but she appeared as eager as Naina to know what had transpired between him and Shyamita.

'Fine,' he said. 'We didn't really talk much, as she was busy unpacking. But we've promised to catch up soon,' he finished.

Neither his mother nor his sister spoke for about ten seconds.

Finally, Naina couldn't take it any longer. 'What? That's it?'

'Well, what were you expecting?' Jai asked her, irritated.

'God! Nothing. Let it be. I can see you are as useless now as you were twelve years ago,' Naina snapped.

'Fine. You go talk to her,' he muttered back. He picked up their suitcases and deposited them in the trunk of his SUV.

'Don't think I won't tell her, Jai,' as always, Naina had to have the last word.

Geet's house was a mad circus. Shyamita had lost count of all the cousins and extended cousins that she was introduced to. Neetu Aunty had introduced her to a lot of Geet's male cousins, whom she considered to be eligible bachelors. It was funny, really. Had it not been for her nervousness, she might have actually had a good time.

But she couldn't. Shyamita Bose was nervous. And her nervousness had nothing to do with all the eligible bachelors. She was nervous because of Jai Nair. One would think that after twelve years of not being in touch, she would have become immune to his presence. But no! Shyamita was still affected by him. Even more now, in fact. Today, she knew the cravings and urges of her body. But she had never thought she would be so deeply affected by Jai's mere presence.

He was standing across the hall, talking to Karan and one of Geet's cousins. His sister, Naina and their mother were right behind him talking to Geet's aunt from Bhatinda.

Their eyes met. Jai smiled. And Shyamita melted.

She could feel the crimson blush on her cheeks.

How can you still do this to me, Jai?

But the man in question seemed oblivious to the effect he was having on her. Flashing his dimples, he excused himself from the conversation he had been having with the two men and gently tapped on his mother's shoulder. He whispered something in her ear and smiling she turned to Naina. The Bhatinda aunty found an uncle from Noida to talk to, and Jai made his way to where Shyamita was standing, his sister and mother in tow.

'Shyamita!' Naina was as vivacious as she had been when she was a little girl. She came over to Shyamita and embraced her in a big hug, kissing her on both cheeks. Jai's mother, Lalita Aunty, also hugged Shyamita. Naina then proceeded to grill Shyamita about life in Paris and about all the other cities where she had lived in the last decade.

'Oh, my god! You've lived in Madrid? I am so jealous.' Naina's voice trailed away, wistful.

'For how long will you be in India, Shyamita?' Lalita Aunty asked.

'For just three weeks, aunty. I am going to Pune after all the functions here are over. I will spend a week at home,' Shyamita replied.

'Oh, that is too short a visit, Shyamita,' Lalita Aunty admonished. 'You must extend your stay and spend some time with us. Naina and I will be in Mumbai for a while before we return to Bangalore.' she added.

'Next time perhaps, aunty,' Shyamita smiled.

Jai watched Shyamita as she spoke to his mother and sister. She had still not spoken to him directly. He knew this trait of hers. She used to do this in school, when she wasn't sure of the answer to a question the teacher asked her, she would simply stare at the walls and blab something.

She looked absolutely beautiful dressed in a long peacock blue skirt, with light brocade work, a lime green sequined top and minimal make-up. Her hair was forced into a knot on the top of her head. But a few tendrils had escaped and were now curled at the nape of her neck. The creamy skin there was just begging to be touched.

But her lips…lush, soft and pink. Jai wanted nothing more than to plant a deep and passionate kiss on her luscious lips. He wanted to spread her hair across a pillow, and have her breathing heavily under him while he kissed her to a frenzied pitch.

Wait…what? Was he seriously he having lascivious thoughts about Mithi? He never had such thoughts about her. What the hell was going on here? She was forbidden territory. *Wasn't she?*

Jai was positive that Shyamita had no idea how much she affected him. And it was this innocence of hers which proved to be a bigger turn-on for him. In his mind, there was nothing sexier than a woman who didn't know the power she wielded over a man.

And then Shyamita did the most shocking thing he had ever seen her do. She looked at him and winked.

Jai had to correct himself. There was nothing sexier than a woman who *knew* the power she wielded over a man.

Shyamita didn't know what it was about Jai but just having him in the same room made all her problems and grievances melt away. She could hear herself laughing at the way Naina was teasing her older brother. She hadn't laughed like this in years.

In a cream kurta-pajama with his wicker moccasins, he looked every bit the bestselling writer. Everyone else had eyes on Karan, the groom. But Shyamita only looked at Jai. She was sure that there were a few girls whispering to each other about him. A couple of older women were also ogling him. In fact, Shyamita was sure that if she hadn't known Jai from school, Neetu Aunty would have introduced him to her as another eligible bachelor. Would she have laughed it off then, like how she had when she was asked to meet the other bachelors? Or would she have thought Jai to be different?

Shyamita's mind was running haywire with all these questions. And for the life of her, she didn't know how to answer even a single one of them. How could she have feelings for Jai when she had just met him? She was over him. She was. She had been in relationships. But had she been in love? She had never let anybody get close enough to ever fall in love.

It had taken a great number of counseling sessions with Geet over the telephone and subsequently over Skype at ungodly hours to get Jai out of her system. During each conversation, Geet would invent a new profanity to throw at Jai and Shyamita in her own way would find out whatever little she could about Jai without being too obvious.

She'd learnt from Geet that after his masters, Jai had returned to India, with two published short-story collections in his kitty. Back in Mumbai, for a short while he lived in a small flat at Andheri. He then moved to Worli, to a slightly more upscale flat. It was somewhere around this time that success finally found him and he wrote three bestsellers in a short span of two years. He now lived on Carter Road and had also bought a small flat for his mother in Bangalore.

So what if she knew so much about him? He was her friend after all. She was bound to know. She knew she couldn't deal with so much so soon. She had only just come back to Mumbai. And she was here for Geet only. She would be back in Paris soon and life would be back to normal again.

What about Jai? A little voice chimed in her head, but she shushed it because just then, Geet called her to her side. Jai was called by Karan. They made their way together to where the couple was standing.

Geet's lehenga-choli was in a shade of gold and cream and she looked absolutely gorgeous. The entire hall had been done up in hues of mellow orange, gold, and cream and standing below an archway made of white roses, Geet and Karan exchanged rings.

Applause rang out across the hall. And as she watched Geet smiling from ear-to-ear, Shyamita felt a small stab of envy.

4

The last of the guests, who were staying in various hotels across the city, finally left. Shyamita really wanted to soak her feet in warm water. She had danced practically all evening. And due to Geet's outrageous choice in music, the DJ played everything – from Hip-Hop and House to Bollywood and Bhangra. But Shyamita hadn't danced like this in ages. Back in Paris, whenever she went clubbing with Mia, they always ended up sitting in a corner of the bar, with Mia flirting with the bartender and Shyamita doodling on the tissue paper.

But there was something about Bollywood music and Bhangra that just pulled you to the dance floor. Even in Paris, the one time she and Mia had been to a discotheque on Bollywood night, they had 'ripped the dance floor', to quote Mia. But now, her friend was heavily pregnant, and so they very rarely went clubbing. In India, however, you can start a club even in your own house, as Geet always said.

When Shyamita had been dragged onto the dance floor by Naina, for a while she had been at a loss for what to do. She knew Jai was watching her. She could feel his eyes on her. Finally, mustering up courage, she looked straight at him. In that instance, Jai gave her his most brilliant smile. He then set his glass down, shook hands with one of Geet's brothers whom he had been talking to and made his way to where she was standing.

For Shyamita, the room and its occupants had pretty much faded away. She had eyes only for him. As he walked toward her, she could feel her pulse rate increasing, her breathing turned shallow and she could feel the short hairs on the nape of her neck standing. She was losing her peripheral vision. Suddenly, she was a Yash Chopra heroine!

And then the DJ played *their* song. It had been their favorite song while in school. They would listen to it on their walkmans all day long, sometimes even during class, much to the ire of their teachers.

Shyamita didn't know whether Jai saw it as a sign, but it gave her the courage to meet him halfway. She placed her hands on her hips and began to do the step they had mastered when they were in school. It was something she thought she had erased from her memory. But, Jai and their song...it all came back to her. They had watched the Shahrukh Khan and Kajol starrer together, right after their ninth grade final examinations. It had been their favorite movie.

Jai laughed when he saw her do *their* step. He matched her step for step. Soon the two of them were dancing their hearts out, and everybody else had stopped to watch them.

Before they knew it, everybody was singing and clapping to the beat.

When the song ended, applause rang through the hall. Shyamita was sure she was as red as a tomato. Beside her, she could see Jai trying to set his hair straight; her peripheral vision had returned. When their eyes met, for the briefest of moments, a sense of contentment spread through her.

But Shyamita knew that she could never be content with the present status quo that she and Jai shared. She had always wanted more. In fact that was why they had parted ways in the first place. And now, as she ascended the stairs that led to her bedroom, she couldn't help but wonder if she wasn't setting herself up for heartbreak again. She knew she couldn't go down that road again. Granted she was much younger then and could have probably handled it better, but even today, when it came to Jairam Nair, all sense and reason seemed to desert her.

And Jai hadn't even given any signs. She didn't even know if he was seeing someone. She knew nothing of his personal life. She made a mental note to ask Geet.

She made a mental note to cancel the earlier mental note.

She couldn't risk falling for Jai again.

In his hotel room, Jai refilled his third glass of chilled apple juice. A teetotaler, he very rarely indulged in late-night introspection. But tonight was that kind of night. So with a glass of chilled juice in his hand, he sat down on the couch in his apartment's living room and pondered over the day's events.

His reaction to Shyamita earlier that evening still shocked him. He couldn't understand the sudden urge he had had to kiss her senseless and leave her gasping for more. But strangely, he was the one being rendered catatonic in her presence. Nothing had prepared him for the assault on his senses the moment she had set foot into the hall earlier. Was he giving her that power? Or was it something that he was allowing to happen to him?

None of this made any sense. He was here for his best friend. Hell, he was his best man. And for the life of him he couldn't figure out why he was stuck on a certain Bengali bombshell. He remembered how her peacock blue skirt had sparkled while they were dancing, and the orange and yellow lights of the hall had seemed to add a mischievous glint to her laughter. But Jai had been mesmerized by her eyes. She had always complained of her eyes being too big for her face.

'Yuck. I look like a tadpole,' she had once said.

'A very pretty tadpole,' he had offered, but only to get kicked in the shin for his remark.

But tonight, his Mithi wasn't a pretty tadpole. She looked stunning. Nothing could have prepared him for the way his body had reacted when he'd seen her as she entered the room. His entire world had tilted. In fact, his world had lost its axis and was teetering dangerously. And it was when Shyamita had caught his eye from across the room, and winked, that he lost track of his world. That's when he had decided that before the night would come to a close, he was going to dance with his *oldest* best friend.

God-damn-it! He was going to have to talk to Shyamita. For his sake. For his peace of mind.

He put his glass down on the table next to his bed. He stood up and looked at his reflection in the French windows. *Not bad*, he thought. He could see the moon outside, a lone star twinkling beside it.

No, he said to himself. The star wasn't alone. It had the moon. She stood there for him. And encouraged by that train of thought, Jai picked up his car keys from the bureau and walked out of his apartment. He was going to get back his moon.

Shyamita couldn't sleep. She was too tightly wound up. She tried reading a book on the newest artists in the sub-continent. She stared at the first sentence for more than seven minutes. She threw the book aside and began to plait her hair. But the curls just couldn't be tamed. So she let them be. Finally, she got out of bed. She thought she'd check her email and see if there were updates from Mia.

Since landing in India, she hadn't spoken to her friend and was now feeling a little guilty. There was one email from Mia asking her if she had reached safely and informing her that the baby was healthy and probably missing his aunt. Shyamita had tears in her eyes as she read Mia's email. Her friend had taken her in when she had been at her lowest. She had been weak, insecure and terribly fragile. But Mia had supported her and been by her side as she had rebuilt her life.

Shyamita knew Mia was staying at Michael's till the time she went back. So she didn't call or Whatsapp her. She replied to her email saying that she had reached safely and that she was missing her precious nephew, too. She wondered if she should tell Mia about what had transpired between her and Jai. But she thought it best not to worry her friend in her present state. She ended the email saying that she would call soon.

Just as she hit the send button, there was a dull thud outside her window. Thinking it was a cat, she didn't pay much heed to it. But then she heard another kind of sound. It sounded like a stone hitting the window. Again. And again.

Shyamita didn't even need to think about who it could be. She knew. She ran to the window, opened it and looked out just as Jai was swinging his arm to throw another pebble.

'Stop! Jai, you'll wake up the whole house,' she whispered as loudly as she could.

'Mithi, come down,' he shouted.

'Shh...no. Jai, go away,' she replied.

'If you're not coming down, then I'll come up,' he retorted and started for the main door.

'No, no. Jai, wait.'

'Are you coming down?'

Shyamita didn't answer. She could hear her own heartbeat in the silence of the night.

'Mithi, I'm going to ring the doorbell. You can field all the questions people will ask,' he shouted again.

And Shyamita gave in. And just like she used to say twelve years ago, she said, 'Jai, I'm coming down.'

She quickly pulled on a pair of blue jeans to wear with her white kurta, and dug out a yellow phulkari scarf from her suitcase, stuffed her feet into jootis and ran down the stairs as quietly as she could. When she reached the main door, she fumbled a bit with all the bolts and latches. Finally, she opened the door. And there stood Jai. Like he always did. Hands in his pocket, head bent down and kicking a tiny pebble.

She quickly closed the door behind her, and asked him like she used to, 'Where to, Jai?'

He smiled, put his arm around her waist and said, 'Marine Drive.'

5

Marine Drive was still as beautiful as it had been all those years ago. In fact, Mumbai had hardly changed. Granted traffic had increased, the rains messed up the city every year, terrorism had tried to rip the city apart, but all in all, Mumbai still stood. And for Shyamita, Mumbai had always been her link to Jai. And Marine Drive always had a special place in her heart. Back in their school days, they would come here on the weekends. They'd spend hours on the beach, by the rocks and would end their day with chaat and kulfi. By the time they would catch the bus to go back to their hostel, night would have descended. The street lights would have come on and the entire stretch appeared like one giant necklace.

Tonight, it was no different. There were just a few people sitting by the rocks. Since it was too dark, people didn't venture down to the lower rocks. The sky was a deep, dark blue; the moon and her sole companion, a star, shone bright. After a while, the clouds partially covered the moon, but the star still managed to shine through.

Jai noticed this arrangement. He wasn't a romantic or anything. But there was a reason behind why he had brought Shyamita here. He had to tell her how he felt. He just had to.

They sat on the topmost rocks. Slightly wet from the waves, the rocks were sticky and sandy, but Shyamita never complained. She would never complain about her clothes getting wet and dirty. Over the years, he had tried bringing a few of his dates to this same spot. But none of them would sit on the rocks, saying that their clothes would get soiled or that the rocks were too sharp. He had missed Shyamita's easygoing and carefree nature. In her white kurta she looked every bit like the simple girl-next-door he had known in his school days. The bright yellow of her phulkari scarf played a sharp contrast to the darkness of the sky. But somehow, instead of unsettling him, the color only helped calm his nerves. He was here for a reason. He needed to speak to Shyamita.

There was a light breeze blowing. Mixed with the saltiness of the sea, it mingled with the night's air and the various smells of Mumbai. Shyamita loved it.

'Oh, how I've missed this,' she sighed softly.

And Jai knew he had taken the right decision by bringing them here.

He tucked a flying tendril of her hair behind her ear and Shyamita turned to look at him. She smiled her soft smile, which had always had the ability to turn him to a giant blob of melting chocolate.

Clearing his throat, he said, 'Mithi, I have to tell you something.'

'Okay.'

'I… er… Mithi, I…,' he fumbled.

'Jai, it's me. You can tell me anything, right?' she asked.

Except this, Jai thought. 'Er, yes. I can tell you anything, Mithi.'

'Then tell me. What is it?'

'Mithi, do you remember the last time we came here?'

And Shyamita stiffened. 'Jai,' she said in a low voice, 'can we not talk about it, please?'

Jai looked at her. She had turned to face the black sea, her posture erect. It was as though she was giving out a warning without words.

'Mithi, we need to,' he ventured.

'No,' was all she said.

People were staring at them. People always stared at them. A boy and a girl in their teens, walking down Marine Drive was hardly a comforting notion for many people. In their minds, the boy and girl were either siblings, or they were children spoilt beyond repair by their parents. But Jai and Shyamita were having the time of their lives. They devoured pani puri and kulfi; sang their favorite songs out loud. They sat down on the rocks and watched the sun set into the sea. The sky was painted a beautiful orange-red.

Shyamita dropped her head on Jai's shoulder and the two of them sat there like that for what felt like hours. But soon, it was time to go back to the hostel.

'Mithi,' Jai whispered. When Shyamita didn't respond, he tapped her lightly on her head and said, 'Mithi, chalo, we have to go.'

Shyamita, groggy and disoriented, lifted her head from Jai's shoulder. The night had engulfed them now, the sky a dark, deep shade of blue. Stars were twinkling happily in the night sky, and the moon was playing peek-a-boo with the clouds. They stood up, Jai helping Shyamita get to her feet. Suddenly, she tripped and almost fell backwards as her foot got caught between the rocks. Jai caught hold of her just in time and pulled her to him.

In that moment, their eyes met and Shyamita's world tilted. Her breath caught and her pulse began to race. She didn't know what took her over, but right then, she wanted to kiss Jai.

And she did. She stretched up on her toes and she kissed her best friend on his mouth. Shyamita was lost. Her hands, of their own volition, wound around his neck, her fingers spread into the curls at his nape. She sighed and moaned softly. She was happy, delirious even. Until she realized that only she was kissing Jai. He wasn't kissing her. In fact, Jai's hands were plastered to his sides. He wasn't even holding her.

Shocked and dismayed at her foolishness, Shyamita pulled herself away from him. Her heart pounding even faster than before, her mouth had gone dry. She couldn't bring herself to look at Jai. And when he turned and walked away, without even helping her walk through the rocks, tears welled up in her eyes.

Shyamita was in tears again. And as they fell down her cheeks, she couldn't wipe them away in time before Jai saw them. And when Jai saw the tears rolling down her cheeks, there was nothing in this world he wanted to do more than hug his best friend. So he did.

He put his left arm around her shoulders and pulled her close to him. Shyamita slid wordlessly into his embrace, resting her head on his shoulder. Her tears ran freely now. Soon there was a wet patch on Jai's shirt, but he didn't care much about it. He brought his other arm around her in a protective gesture, and she let him enfold her in his arms. Her tears had stopped by now and they just sat like that on the rocks.

Finally he said, 'Mithi…'

'Hmmm…' came her reply.

'Mithi, I am so sorry. I messed up.'

She didn't say anything for a while. The silence of the night was unnerving. And Jai was about to have a nervous breakdown when Shyamita finally said, 'Jai, can you kiss me *now*?'

6

It was something that should have happened a long time ago. And as Jai lowered his head to kiss her, at that moment, everything in his life fell magically into place. There was nowhere else he needed to be. There was nobody else he wanted to be with. This, here and now, was all he wanted.

Her scent was absolutely mesmerizing. A soft blend of vanilla and lilac, Jai was lost already. So when his lips finally touched hers, everything inside him exploded. He drove his fingers into her tangled mane and deepened the kiss. Her soft velvety mouth presented itself like ambrosia to him. Biting slowly into the soft, lush pad of her lower lip, he let his arms fall down to her waist and almost crushed her with a force that could have knocked the breath out of her.

But it was her passion that took him aback completely. She matched him every step of the way. Her fingers plunged into his hair, and her breasts were pushed up against his chest. She tugged him harder to herself and deepened the kiss by opening her mouth and allowing his tongue to enter. What followed was like an ancient rhythmic dance, the rush of waves providing the music.

Finally, gasping for breath, Jai reluctantly pulled away from her. He gently cupped her face in his hands and said, 'I believe it was Rolf Edberg who said it is only by the sea that we can see into ourselves. And I can *see into* myself clearly now, Mithi. This is what I have always wanted. You and me…by the sea. It's like our very own mistletoe.'

Shyamita didn't know what to say. The words Jai had just spoken, so poignant, so precious.... She couldn't articulate a response. So she did what she had wanted to do for a very long time. She hugged Jairam Nair.

And when his arms came around her, Shyamita was home. Even the sea seemed to have noticed and understood this quiet exchange. It stopped thrashing about recklessly, the waves gently and calmly hitting the rocks.

Shyamita and Jai stayed like that for a long time. As they looked out to the sea, they realized that there wasn't any other place in this world they'd rather be at this moment. Everything they wanted was right there. As the sun finally made its appearance, painting the sky a magnificent gold, Shyamita lifted her head from Jai's shoulder.

'Jai, we should go. Geet…'

When Jai turned to look at her their eyes met and another thread of magic started to weave around them. Jai bent his head down, Shyamita's breath caught, their lips met and everything else was forgotten again.

It was nearly eight in the morning when Jai and Shyamita finally made their way back to Geet's house. That nobody was awake was proof that last night had indeed been spectacular. A party in a Punjabi household meant that everyone, practically everyone, would have had more than a little too much to drink.

'Coffee?' Shyamita whispered softly.

Jai nodded. They made their way to the kitchen, where Shyamita prepared coffee while Jai rummaged about for some bread and jam. Not able to find anything, he cut two slices of the cake from last night, which he found in the refrigerator. A small breakfast table had been installed on the terrace that adjoined the kitchen. And it was here that Shyamita and Jai had their morning coffee along with two delicious slices of cake.

And it was here that Geet found them nearly forty-five minutes later.

'Arre waah! Jairam Nair and Shyamita Bose. Is there something I should know about?'

Shyamita spilled the last bit of coffee on her white kurta, ruining it for life. She looked towards Jai, but he didn't seem to be ruffled by Geet's presence at all.

'Hello Bridezilla,' he teased.

'Shut up,' Geet muttered. 'What are you two doing here, anyway?' She continued her investigation.

'Geet, we...uhh...I...uhh...,' Shyamita didn't know what to say.

The sudden buzzing of Jai's cell phone saved them both from answering anymore of Geet's questions. *Saved by the bell*, thought Shyamita.

'It's Karan,' Jai informed the girls.

'Hey, bro, what's up?'

Where the bloody hell are you, Jairam Nair? Karan's voice was so loud and booming that Shyamita could hear it even though Jai had not turned on the speakerphone.

'I am at Geet's place. I just came to drop off Mithi,' Jai winked at Shyamita.

Drop Mithi? Why? Where did the two of you go?

Beside her, Shyamita could feel Geet's curiosity pouring out of every pore in her body. She knew her friend was itching to know all the juicy details. Damn Jai for putting her in a spot like this. She knew she would have to answer all of Geet's questions, and there would be hundreds, after Jai left.

'Relax bro. I am on my way. See you in twenty.'

Jai disconnected the call, calmly drank the last of his coffee, and said, 'Okay girls. I've got to go. I'll see you two in the evening.'

And he left.

Shyamita wanted to kill Jai, but she settled for dreaming about him. No sooner had he left than she made excuses about her head aching and escaped to the sanctuary of her room before Geet began her tirade of questions. Shyamita knew she would have to face the music eventually but right now she was just not in the mood.

And now as she lay down on the soft duvet, she thought about Jai and their night together. Everything had been so perfect. Magical.

The sea is our mistletoe. What a lovely and reassuring thought. Her writer man evidently knew his way with words.

Wait a minute. Jai was a writer, yes. But was he her man too? As her brain tried to logically formulate an answer to that, her eyes began to droop and before long, Shyamita was dreaming about kisses, waves, mistletoes and yes, her man.

'Dude, what are you doing with Shyamita?' Karan cornered Jai the moment they were alone in the line at the breakfast buffet.

'What do you mean?' Jai looked at him quizzically.

'I mean is there somewhere you're going with this? Or are you just having fun with her for now?' Karan asked and quickly began piling sausages onto his plate, but not before Jai noticed his sheepish expression.

'That ever-inquisitive fiancée of yours put you up to this, right?' Jai bristled.

'Well...er...yes, kind of. But I want to know, too.'

'Well, both you and your precious fiancée need to back off. This is between me and Shyamita. And I'm sure we are old enough to handle this.'

And with that, Jai stomped off to his table. He set his plate down noisily and managed to get a questioning look from his sister.

'What is it?' he asked her, slowly beginning to see red.

'Nothing,' Naina replied, knowing her brother was in no mood to be asked where he had been all night. Although, she knew exactly with whom her brother had been last night.

As a little girl, Geet Chadda had always dreamed of a big fat wedding with loads of dancing, music and, yes, gifts too! But tonight, despite the fact that she was going to be married to the man of her dreams in four days, Geet was worried. And as she paced the length of her room dressed in her beautiful baby pink ghaghra-choli with silver sequins, beads and motifs, she had only one thought on her mind: Shyamita.

Geet and Shyamita had practically been sisters when they were in school. But Geet had always resented Shyamita's closeness to Jai. She had never been able to understand what her friend saw in him. She had known then that her friend was crazily in love with him. But Geet had never been too happy about it. According to Geet, Jai was much too arrogant for his own good. And so when the two had gone their separate ways, Geet had silently rejoiced thinking that her friend would finally be able to find someone better suited and worthy of her. But to Geet's utter dismay, when she had called Shyamita in Paris to invite her for the wedding, her friend's first question had been, 'Who all will be there from school?'

Geet had replied exasperatedly, 'Just a few of our close friends, Shyamu.'

'Wasn't Karan very close to Jai in school?'

'Yes,' Geet bristled, 'Nair will be there, too.'

'Geet! Be nice,' Shyamita had admonished.

Over the years, she'd grown to like Jai. But she still wasn't sure whether he was the man for her dear friend. But she also knew that Shyamita hadn't smiled and had fun in years. This was why she had taken Jai up to Shyamita's room the day before. She had wanted to see how her friend would react. And Shyamita had reacted exactly the way Geet had predicted. She had fumbled and stuttered and blushed. She was still crazily in love with the idiot.

Yes, the girl lived in Paris, the city of love. But she knew Shyamita. She would never actively seek someone, because the foolish girl believed that she wasn't pretty enough or some such nonsense.

'But the truth is, Shyamu,' Geet mused aloud, 'You're gorgeous. You're free and beautiful.'

And right there, at that moment, Geet Chadda made two secret vows to her girlfriend. Firstly, she would always be there to protect her from any harm that was likely to come her way because of Jairam Nair. And secondly, if her friend suffered from another heartbreak, she, Geet Chadda, would kill Jairam Nair!

She smiled to herself, satisfied with her vows. She walked towards her bedroom door and was just about to open it when her cell phone rang. She frowned when she read the caller-ID. It was Jai. *Why on earth is he calling me?* She wondered as she answered.

7

'Shit! Where the hell are those earrings?' Shyamita cursed as she rummaged about the room for her earrings. She was running late and Geet was going to kill her. The function had started fifteen minutes ago and twice already, Geet had sent Raman Kaka, the Chadda family's oldest, most faithful and toothless servant, to call her. Shyamita had always loved the old man. When she used to visit after school, she would tease him about his teeth and tell him how handsome he looked even though he didn't have any. The old man would just laugh it off, pat her head, and set in front of her a large plate of the most delicious pakodas. But today, she had no time to tease him. She had looked everywhere and still hadn't been able to find her earrings. She was sure she had kept them out along with her clothes and other accessories before going for a shower. *Where the hell were they?*

Finally, she gave up. She checked her appearance in the mirror one last time before she headed downstairs. She liked what she saw. *I only hope Jai likes what he sees, too*, she thought and walked out of her room, still cursing the missing earrings.

Jai was utterly and absolutely mesmerized when he saw Shyamita walk into the party. She was dressed in a beautiful cream sari, with a red and gold border, small crystals studded across the entire body of the sari and a long sleeved red blouse, which had the same crystals around the cuffs. A beautiful ruby and crystal choker was around her neck, her hair was set in waves around a face that was of a dancer – eyes drawn and lined with the darkest of kohl, her cheekbones were defined by a light blush, and her lips were dipped in the same deep red of her sari. But Jai's attention had been drawn to the red and gold jeweled cummerbund circling her waist. *Oh, my god,* he thought.

She was stunning!

And Jai was sure every man in the party was of the same opinion. Shyamita's entry had created quite a stir and almost everyone in the garden, for that was where the party was being held, turned to stare at her. Some of the men were looking at her like she was something to be devoured. Jai wanted to wipe the drool of their chins and then proceed to wipe the floor with them. He reigned in his temper and simply walked over to where Shyamita was talking to his mother and sister.

When he reached them, he slowly slid his hand around Shyamita's creamy waist of which she was giving everybody a tantalizing glimpse. God! He wanted to eat her up. He was aware of her reaction to him. He heard her breath catch and saw her eyes flare, first in surprise and then with a feeling he only knew too well when he was around her. *Desire*. And then she leaned slightly to her right and rested against him. This time Jai's breath caught and it took everything he had in him to not pull her away, up the Chaddas' bungalow and into her bedroom; remove every item of clothing she wore, reveal the ambrosia beneath and just sink himself into her.

Controlling his wayward thoughts, or at least trying to, he cut into the discussion the women were having about Naina going to stay with Shyamita over next summer for her exchange program. 'Amma, could I just steal Mithi away for two minutes?'

His mother nodded earnestly and his sister winked at him. *Gosh! Those two were going to have to be given lessons on what is subtle and what is not.* He steered Shyamita away from them and took her to a small bench that was on the other side of the garden. He knew that every man in the party was cursing him right at this moment and Jairam Nair was enjoying that feeling. Shyamita was all his. That is how it was supposed to have been right from the start. And he was going to do everything he could to make it happen. He was going to make the girl he had fallen in love with all those years ago, fall in love with him.

With that thought firmly planted in his head, he sat her down gently on the bench and sat beside her.

'I think every guy at the party is cursing me to hell right now,' he said.

She looked at him, her big beautiful eyes expressing her confusion, 'why will they curse you, Jai?'

'Because I have the most beautiful girl by my side,' he replied, and Shyamita blushed.

Jai took her hand in his. Squeezing it gently, he said, 'Mithi, I...I...you....' Words failed him; ironic considering he was a bestselling author and poet. But this woman had acquired a way of making him short of breath and words. He looked down at their hands twined together and felt a serious pang of longing. He had so much to say, but he just was not able to articulate himself. To his surprise and utter delight, Shyamita placed her other hand on top of his and gave it a gentle squeeze, as though egging him on to speak. He looked up at her to see that she was smiling a radiant and jubilant smile and her eyes were sparkling. Jai's heart almost burst at the seams. He smiled, and filched out a rectangular-shaped box from the inside pocket of his jacket and placed it in her right hand.

Shyamita looked down at the pale green box Jai had placed in her hand. Her heart began to beat wildly. *What was inside the box?* She looked up at Jai in the hopes of finding answers in his eyes, but he just said, 'Open it, Mithi.'

And she did. Inside was a breathtakingly beautiful and intricately designed pair of ruby and pearl drop earrings, with a small heart-shaped diamond in the centre. 'Oh, my God! Jai…' was all Shyamita could manage.s

'Jai… I can't take this. It's too much,' she whispered as tears began to well in her eyes.

Jai smiled and whispered, 'Mithi, I have so much that I wish to say to you. But for some strange reason, I'm not able to articulate my feelings. I will get there, I promise. In the meantime though, consider these earrings as my way of telling you how invaluably precious you are to me.'

This time, Shyamita couldn't stop her tears from escaping. And amidst tears and smiles, Jai fastened the earrings onto Shyamita's earlobes and drew back to see how she looked.

'Beautiful. And more importantly… mine,' he pronounced emphatically.

And for Shyamita, that was the moment she chose to fall in love with Jairam Nair all over again.

'Shyamu, where did you disappear to?' Geet demanded just as Shyamita and Jai rejoined the rest of the party in the garden.

'I was just…' before she could finish, Jai put his hand around Shyamita's waist and said, 'She was with me, Geet.'

Geet ignored him and asked Shyamita, 'Are you alright? You look like you've cried. Did he say something? I can have Karan throw him out right now,' she finished.

'What the hell is your problem, Geet?' Jai blasted.

'My problem is you, Jairam Nair. And just because I helped you with the color of her sari so you could get matching earrings, doesn't mean you're in my good books,' Geet rebutted.

'Wait a minute…' Shyamita blurted. 'Geet, you hid my earrings?'

But Geet didn't say anything. She stomped off in a fit of temper.

Shyamita turned to look up at Jai, 'Did you two plan this?'

'Yes, Mithi,' Jai replied. 'I called that scatter-brain and asked her to help me with the color of your sari for this evening.'

Shyamita had to smile. 'You know she's not your biggest fan and you still called her. Why?'

'Because I wanted to surprise you, even if that meant that I had to talk to the most difficult person on the planet,' he added.

'Thank you, Jai,' Shyamita managed, close to tears again.

'Hey! Can we put a stop to those tears for a while? I don't want Indian blondie's Ken doll to throw me out.'

'He's your best friend, Jai.'

'He is. Although I don't know what he sees in…,' Shyamita punched him lightly on his chest, 'Ow! Okay, okay. Let's go get something to drink!'

When you are at a Punjabi wedding you can be sure of one thing – there is no limit to the amount of fun you can have. Almost everybody would hit the dance floor at the same time. Loud Bollywood and Bhangra music would bellow from the gigantic speakers. Enough food would be piled onto your plate for you to suffer from indigestion the next morning. By the end of the night, not only would your soles ache from all that dancing, but you would have consumed enough alcohol to last you an entire lifetime.

The Chaddas were one of the wealthiest Punjabi families and one of the oldest in the jewelry business. Three generations of the family had lived in the heart of Mumbai city, in the same mansion. When Geet's father took over the family business, he renovated the older parts of the house, keeping its old charm intact, installed some of the latest state-of-the-art luxuries in the newer wings, and even re-landscaped the gardens.

So naturally Geet's wedding had to be different. In the sense, it had to be more. Therefore, apart from the usual hullabaloo that is expected at a Sangeet, there were choreographed dances performed by couples and groups from both the bride and groom's families. Old uncles and aunties crooned and ultimately croaked into the microphones and children were made to show off their 'talents' by their parents. It was close to 10 p.m. when Geet and Karan finally made their way onto the dance floor to dance to their song. And in typical Bollywood style, Karan got down on one knee and proposed to the woman of his dreams in front of both the families and with the screen in the background showing montages of various Yash Chopra films.

'I think I am going to gag any minute now,' Jai whispered to Shyamita. They were both seated close to the stage and had been watching all the action unfold in silence.

'Shh…,' she hushed and giggled. 'This is how Geet had always wanted it, Jai. You know her.'

'Yeah, well…I know Karan too. And I'm shocked that he doesn't mind doing all this drama,' Jai responded.

Shyamita took a deep breath before saying, 'Love makes you do strange things, Jai. Things which would have initially been anathema to you, just seem to come so naturally when you are in love.'

Jai looked at her with a puzzled expression on his face. 'C'mon, Mithi,' he said, 'how can you believe that? Honestly?'

'Why not?' she asked.

'Mithi, love is not about changing yourself for somebody else, right? Don't you lose yourself in the process?'

'No, Jai. You are looking at all this very clinically. When you fall in love you will know what I'm talking about,' she ended.

Jai did not respond to that. Instead he sat quietly mulling over what Shyamita had just said. Was love going to change him, too? Would he start behaving like Karan? *Dear God!*

Parents with babies and little children were the first to leave. They were slowly followed by the old uncles and aunties, tired after their vocal excursions. Nearly eight to nine minibuses left the Chadda residence and transported the guests to their respective hotels. Geet and Shyamita sat on the swing in the garden, both a little tipsy from all the celebratory champagne.

'Shyamu, can I ask you something?' Geet began.

Shyamita looked at her friend with a puzzled expression on her face before blurting, 'Since when did Geet Chadda need my permission before interrogating me?'

Geet giggled. Shyamita giggled. It was as though they were back in high school.

'Fine. I'll just go ahead and say what I have to,' Geet said finally.

'Okay!' Shyamita replied.

'Shyamu, I don't want you falling for Jai again,' Geet started. When Shyamita did not say anything in response, Geet continued, 'The guy is just not right for you. You need somebody who will bring stability and happiness into your life. You deserve that. You don't need someone like Jai. He's not right for you, Shyamu.'

'Why isn't he right for me, Geet?' Shyamita had to know.

Geet looked hesitantly at her closest and oldest friend. How could she tell her that Jairam Nair was trouble from the word go? Geet knew Jai's family background, Karan had told her everything. Personally she was very happy that Jai had come out of the trauma and made something of himself. But she didn't want her friend to be a part of all that. Shyamita had been through enough without Jai bringing more complications into her life.

Before she could articulate a response to that, the men came up behind them saying, 'Hello, ladies! How high are we?'

Again, both the girls giggled and turned around to face them, their incomplete conversation forgotten.

8

With the last of the wedding guests departing, Shyamita watched as Karan lifted an almost asleep Geet into his arms and carried her into the house. She was happy for Geet, she truly was. But somewhere deep down, she couldn't help but feel a certain pang of envy. Her friend had found true love. She knew that the couple had faced a lot of objections to their union despite the fact that Karan was from an equally loud and boisterous Punjabi family.

But after nearly six years of convincing both the families, Geet and Karan were finally coming together. It was a beautiful story. And the fact that it was turning a new in both their lives made the story all the more beautiful.

Shyamita wanted this too. At least she had wanted this at one point. But now...*what did she want now?*

She turned around to see Jai talking softly into his cell phone. He was talking quickly and every now and then would rake his fingers through his hair. Was everything alright? Whom was Jai talking to? Wasn't it too late?

Shyamita tried her level best not to let these questions bother her. But now that the effects of alcohol were wearing off, she tried to recall the conversation she had had with Geet just an hour or so ago. She couldn't remember the particulars really, but she knew that Geet had asked her not to fall for Jai. But why? What did her friend mean?

And then suddenly, the air was filled with a soft melody. Her thoughts abandoned, Shyamita watched as Jai walked towards her, the music playing from his iPhone. She recognized the tune just as he stopped in front of her. James Blunt sang '*You're beautiful*', as did Jairam Nair. And Shyamita threw her head back and laughed.

To Jai, it was the most beautiful sight, watching his Mithi laugh her heart out. So he sang some more and she laughed some more.

'Guys, you mind keeping it down? It's almost 3 a.m. and I somehow managed to put the loudest Chadda to sleep,' Karan's voice broke into the moment.

Shyamita quickly apologized. 'It's okay, Shyamu. You don't have to apologize for having a good time, you know. So relax, hmm.'

Jai, annoyed at being left out of the conversation, said in an acerbic tone to Karan, 'Don't you have to get some beauty sleep, lover boy?'

'Errr…relax, Nair. There's smoke coming out of your ears,' he replied.

Jai felt like shooting Karan between the eyes right then. Instead he said, 'You want to go or shall I send you back to the hotel in pieces?'

'Don't sweat it, old man. I'm out of here,' came Karan's response. But just before getting into his Audi A6, he called out to Shyamita, 'Oii...Shyamu, you really are beautiful!'

Shyamita blushed; Karan winked and sped off before Jai could hurl a brick from the garden bed at his car.

'I am going to kill that moron when I see him at the hotel,' Jai muttered.

Shyamita's face fell. 'You're leaving now?' she asked.

Jai looked at Shyamita. She was so beautiful in her cream sari. She had tied her hair up into a chignon when Jai had gifted her with the earrings. His heart filled with pride. She was something else. And even now as she looked up at him with her big chocolate brown eyes, her face still recovering from all the blushing she had been doing throughout the evening, her crimson painted lips parted slightly, all he wanted to do was kiss her right there and then.

'No, sweetheart,' he said, before crushing her in his arms.

Shyamita melted in Jai's arms. This was where she had wanted to be all evening. She hadn't been able to take her eyes off him all evening. Dressed in a black, golden-flecked dhoti-kurta, black mojris, with light stubble grazing his jaw line and his unruly long hair combed all the way back and tied with a small black ribbon – he looked like a modern-day Adonis. She had even commented about the ponytail to his sister, Naina. The two girls had laughed about it, but Jai's mother hadn't seemed too happy with her son's rakish looks. 'He thinks he looks very dashing,' she had muttered. But to Shyamita, he was the most gorgeous man she had ever met.

Even now as Jai held her in his arms, his mouth devouring hers, she couldn't help but wish that this moment would last forever. This night should last forever. She loved him. She had always loved him. But Jai...did he love her too? Why had Geet warned her not to fall for him?

Shyamita didn't have time to think as Jai's fingers quickly dislodged her bun and her curls tumbled down. He deepened the kiss and simultaneously his hand moved to her bare waist, pulling her closer to him. Shyamita's breath caught and before she knew it, her hands had moved of their own volition and were now roving up his back. Her fingers quickly pulled his ribbon out, and moved into his hair. Despite the fact that she was wearing killer heels, she had to stretch up to kiss him better. As their tongues met, she pressed her breasts against his chest. Jai's fingers were working their magic at her waist and pressed into the small of her back. His hands came to the front of her sari, and he was about to pull out the pleats when the lights in the garden went out. The watchman must have obviously shut off all the lights now that the party was over.

But that was enough for Shyamita to pull herself out of Jai's embrace. Her heart was racing, and she was pretty sure she had forgotten how to breathe. The dim lights from the street were just about enough for Jai to watch Shyamita. Nervous and fidgety, she was fixing her sari and trying to gather all her curls back into the bun. A nervous giggle escaped her lips and she looked up at Jai, suddenly conscious. But to Jai, it was the cutest sound he had ever heard and he smiled at Shyamita before saying, 'What?'

'What what?' Came Shyamita's reply.

'Can you stand still for just two minutes, Shyamita Bose?' he teased.

'Can you keep your hands off me for two minutes, Jairam Nair?' came her reply. But the impact of what she had said, hit her and her face turned red before she covered her face with her hands.

'Oh, c'mon,' Jai laughed and pulled her to him once again, 'you know the answer to that.'

'Jai,' Shyamita tried to wriggle free of his arms, but he only pulled her in tighter. 'Jai, let me go. Somebody will see us…'

'Who will, Mithi? Everyone is piss drunk and therefore passed out. They're not going to wake up before tomorrow afternoon. As for Sherlock Holmes's female counterpart, she seems to have lost all conscious thought at the moment. Sooo…who will see?'

'Shut up, Jai. Don't be mean,' Shyamita replied amidst giggles.

'Yeah yeah. Okay, let's do something now,' he said.

'Now?' Wide-eyed, she said, 'It's three in the morning, Jai.'

'So what? We can still go.'

'Jai…it's too late.'

'Shh! It's not. There's something I want to show you. Please, Mithi?' Jai was insistent.

Resigned, she said, 'Okay, but let me first change out of my sari,' and tried to wriggle out of his arms again.

Jai tightened his hold on her and said, 'No. Don't. Let's not waste time.'

Shyamita sighed, nodding her acquiescence. Jai finally let her out of his arms, but he slipped his hand into hers and held on tightly. Shyamita looked up into Jai's eyes and smiled. He smiled back; and just like that, they had one of *their* moments again.

They walked hand-in-hand to the parking area where Jai had parked his car. Only it wasn't a car. It was a motorcycle.

'Jai?' Shyamita couldn't disguise the doubt in her voice.

'Yes, sweetheart?'

'I can't sit on this. It's too high. Plus, I'm wearing a sari.'

'So what?'

'Will you just stop with that 'so what'! It's not funny,' she bristled.

'Mithi, it's not that high. And you can sit sideways. You see? No problem at all,' he said in a very smug tone, as if he had just provided a solution to global warming.

Shyamita looked at Jai like as if he had grown not just a second head, but probably a third too.

'I can't sit like that, Jai. Please let me go up and change,' she begged.

'No. You either come in this sari, or you don't come at all,' he said with grave finality.

Shyamita's expression changed to quiet resignation as she tied her unruly curls into a bun again. 'Fine,' she said, 'you're still as stubborn as you were before, Jairam Nair.'

He grinned, and pulled out his KTM Duke 390 from its spot. He gave Shyamita his helmet to wear, but when she looked at him with a *you-really-think-I-am-going-to-wear-that* expression, he simply fitted the helmet onto her head and adjusted the buckle.

She was a sight to behold, in her cream and red sari, with all her baubles sparkling, the matte black helmet, and sporting an expression which said that she was ready to kill him. He quickly sat astride on his motorcycle before she gave way to temptation and really did kill him. He tilted the motorcycle slightly to the left so that Shyamita could sit.

It wasn't easy seating herself sideways. Her sari kept coming in the way as she nearly lost her footing. And the fact that the motorcycle was a tad taller as compared to the others didn't really help her cause. That and the fact that she had a huge helmet sitting on her head at the moment. Finally she managed to seat herself and clenched both hands together in her lap.

'Comfortable?' he asked her.

'As comfortable I can be with all this on me,' Shyamita replied.

'Okay. Let's go then.'

As soon as he revved up his motorcycle, Shyamita let out a small, barely audible squeal. They had hardly moved out of the gate when she let out another squeal.

He killed the motor and asked her, 'Mithi, are you okay?'

'Umm...yeah, I'm fine, Jai,' came her weak response.

'I think you should hold on to me,' he said, a little too eagerly.

Shyamita who was already half leaning on Jai, quickly pulled herself up, and in a voice that betrayed her said, 'Err...no. I'm okay.'

'Mithi, it's a long ride to Carter Road. I think it'd be best if you held on to me,' he added.

'Carter Road?' she looked at him, puzzled.

'Yes, that's where we are going,' came his not so informative response.

'Why are we going to Carter Road, Jai?' she asked, now exasperated.

'Because I want to show you something.' Again, not so informative.

'Oh, my god! Okay,' she said, and leaning into his back put her right hand around his waist.

'You've got to hold on tighter, Mithi,' he insisted.

Shyamita, who would probably combust any minute now, tightened her hold on Jai. He waited for her to settle, then revved up the motorcycle again and they were off.

9

Mumbai at night was stunning. The streets were not teeming with people as it was during the day. There were fewer vehicles, and the street lights danced a merry tune in the moonlight. The sea could be heard all throughout the city as she crashed onto the rocks. The night had its own orchestra of sounds which made the city stand out even more. There were no blaring of horns and polluting vehicles. At night, Mumbai made up for all the discomfort and hassles of the day.

Shyamita would have been able to enjoy all the sights and sounds of the night much better had she not been so focused on not falling off Jai's motorcycle. Geet's house was in Worli. And Worli to Carter Road was a good forty-five-minute ride. But Jai on his motorcycle probably thought he could make it in less than twenty minutes. No conversation was possible as she had to hold on for dear life. Another time perhaps she would have enjoyed the ride immensely. But right now, her sari and the fact that she was sitting sideways only added to her growing discomfort. She wondered if the man moonlighted as a racer when he was not too busy churning out bestsellers.

She didn't have enough time to linger over these thoughts as Jai turned right into a lane, just a few meters after Sachin Tendulkar's 'Bat of honor'. Thick and lush green trees lined both sides of the lane. The moonlight filtered between branches to mix with the streetlights to give the pathway a warm soothing glow.

At the end of it was a large iron gate. Once he reached it, Jai whisked out a small remote from his kurta's side pocket and pressed a green button on it.

Shyamita looked up from her pillion seat and saw an impressive high-rise structure that rose as far as her eyes could see. When the gates opened, Jai sped down the concrete roadway, and turned left into a garage where his four-wheel drive was already parked. He killed the engine of his motorcycle and tilted it to the left again so that Shyamita could get down. Once she did, he straightened up, turned off the lights and got off. He put the motorcycle on its side-stand, before turning to look at Shyamita. She quickly adjusted her sari - the pleats had shifted slightly because of the ride. She then unbuckled the helmet and handed it to Jai. Finally looking up at him she said, 'Jai?'

'Yes, sweetheart?'

'I'd like you to take me on your motorcycle again, only I want to be better dressed,' she said.

'What's wrong with the way you're dressed now?' he teased.

She punched him on his arm. He smiled and said, 'Come.'

From what Shyamita could make out, it was a fairly new building by Mumbai's standards. Not more than ten years old, she guessed. They stepped out of the garage and made their way to the lobby area of the building which was brightly lit with LED lights.

The elevator pinged and Shyamita breathed a huge sigh of relief as she walked into it. As soon as the doors closed, she launched, 'Why are we here, Jai? What is this place?'

Jai took a deep breath before saying, 'This is my house, Mithi.'

But when he said this, Shyamita noticed that his voice shook. He was staring at the floor of the elevator. Shyamita knew that he was having a hard time trying to keep a lid on his emotions. *But why?* She wondered.

The elevator pinged, alerting that they had reached the thirty-third floor.

'Come,' he said, voice thick with emotion. He offered her his hand and Shyamita slid her hand into his wondering at the sudden change of mood. Jai had gone from being cheerful to sombre.

She stepped out of the elevator into a sprawling foyer. The white marble was replaced by dark grey. Soft white LED lights from the ceiling gave the foyer a warm glow despite the grey marble. They walked across to the only door on the floor.

Jai let go of Shyamita's hand and dug out his keys from his pocket. Unlocking the door, he pushed down the handle and turned to Shyamita, hesitant.

'Jai, what is it?' she asked him, her voice reflecting her worry and concern at the way Jai's demeanor had suddenly changed.

'Nothing. C'mon, let's go in.' He slipped his hand into hers again, kissed her lightly on her forehead and pulled her into his apartment. Shyamita followed his lead quietly, still a little worried.

Jai shut the door behind them and stepped into the living room of the house which he had worked so hard to acquire. It had been his dream for so many years, and now finally his dream was turning into reality. The past was going to be just that – the past. His mother and sister were no longer a part of the hellhole. They were free. All those miserable years of his childhood would soon be behind him and they would all start afresh together.

He turned to look at Shyamita who was looking at him with a worried expression on her face. He smiled and pulled her close to his side.

Shyamita's arms coming around his waist was a complete surprise to him. His heart swelled and his happiness reached greater heights.

'Mithi?'

'Hmm?' she murmured as she nuzzled closer to him.

'Would you like a tour?' he asked and kissed the top of her head.

Shyamita nodded enthusiastically.

Jai had rented the sixteenth floor of Belvedere Towers on Carter Road. The apartment had three bedrooms, a sprawling living and dining area, and a wonderfully cosy kitchen. The floor was white marble and the walls painted a simple cream. In the living room, a three and two-seater L-shaped couch in dark beige with silk cushions in bright yellow and red added color, along with a buttery yellow, upholstered loveseat made from the darkest rosewood. Huge floor cushions in bright colors were strewn across the room and in the centre of the room was a plush rug in beige. A small coffee table in the same dark rosewood as the loveseat was placed in the middle of the rug, and was matched by the end tables that were placed on the side of the couch and on both sides of the loveseat.

On one wall of the room were shelves for books and knick-knacks. Shyamita saw some artifacts from Kerala, like the forehead banner of an elephant, called *nettipottu*, and some brass vessels on some of the shelves. There were also souvenirs from countries like Australia, Singapore, Japan, Brazil, Italy, to name a few. Jai had probably bought these during the course of his travels to all these countries for the publicity campaigns of his books. In the middle of all this was a huge LED TV, with a JBL home theatre system, and a dock for an iPod.

The dining area had a simple glass-top oval square table in a deep ebony shade, equipped to seat four persons, and a small low-slung divan in one corner with Japanese-art-inspired upholstery. The living and dining rooms had huge ceiling to floor windows that were adorned with sheer lemon yellow drapes in the lightest of silks. The kitchen was a chef's paradise - huge and equipped with all the possible modern appliances. With Jai's sister studying to become a pastry-chef, this kitchen would probably be heaven for her. Shyamita, who prided herself on her cooking, was tempted to prepare something in that heavenly kitchen. *Maybe someday you will*, a small voice quipped in her head. She shut that voice down before it got the better of her.

Jai was not done with the tour of the house. The first bedroom was for his mother. It had a small terrace garden as well as a small prayer room. The second bedroom was his sister's. And she had been given free rein to do whatever she wanted. So Naina had converted her room into a mini-kitchen for all her experiments in cooking and baking. She too had a terrace garden which she had enclosed from all sides and the top was covered with fibre glass. So the terrace had been converted to a bedroom. 'According to her,' Jai said, 'there is no better way to spend the night than under the stars.' And Shyamita couldn't agree with her more.

The third bedroom was Jai's. At the passage outside his bedroom, Shyamita was assailed by the scent of old parchment and ink. The writing table which sat on the far end of the verandah was probably as old as he was. 'My grandfather's,' Jai said when he saw Shyamita running her fingers through the old wooden-top table. Its edges were frayed and the table top itself had a lot of scars and marks, probably from the compass or divider of a child's geometry set. On the table was a small yellow-bulb lamp with a cream colored lampshade and silver stem. There were several notebooks, loose sheets of paper, and copies of old classics and novels strewn across the table-top. On one corner of the table were several odd-sized penholders crammed with pens and pencils. Four ink bottles sat next to the penholders. On the floor, next to the table were an old typewriter and a laptop – both of which had seen better days.

'Well...this is where I work,' Jai said. He was watching her with keen interest. Never before had he brought a woman home. But with Shyamita, everything just seemed to be so natural, effortless and easy even.

'How long have you been living in this house, Jai?' she asked.

'Just about five months, I think. I moved here after I got my advance on my seventh novel,' came his response. He knew what she was going to ask next.

'Then why aren't Lalita Aunty and Naina staying here?' Shyamita was obviously curious.

10

'Mithi, I am staying at the hotel so that I can be close to Karan and the rest of the wedding party,' he offered.

But Shyamita didn't seem convinced by his answer and said, 'and what about Lalita Aunty and Naina?'

Jai moved closer to where she was standing, took her hands in his and said, 'They haven't really lived here, Mithi. Amma is in Bangalore for almost eight to ten months in a year. And Naina, as you know, is completing her hotel management course in Ahmedabad,' he said before adding, 'and I just started living here a few months ago. In fact, Naina was here for the first two months during her summer break.'

'Jai…I don't know. There's something you're not telling me,' Shyamita was still not convinced. 'Is everything okay?' she asked. 'Who was on the phone when we were at Geet's?'

Jai immediately stiffened. He let go of her hands and raked his fingers through his hair. This was exactly what he had feared. She would start asking him questions he wasn't comfortable answering. Hell, he didn't know what to say. Deep down he knew her confusion was justified. Of course his mother and sister should be staying with him. But they weren't. And her questions weren't making it easier. How could he tell her the sordid details of his family life? He couldn't.

'Jai, tell me. What is the matter?'

'Nothing is the matter, Shyamita! Will you just let it go?' he screamed.

And this time it was Shyamita who stiffened.

Neither said anything. Shyamita just kept staring at Jai. And he looked down at the floor, trying to control his emotions from flying through the roof.

After what seemed like ages, Jai finally looked up and into Shyamita's eyes. What she saw in his eyes nearly shook the earth from beneath her feet. *Tears!*

'Jai?' She made to move towards him but Jai took two steps back. He blinked several times to stop the tears from escaping.

What was wrong? Shyamita wanted to ask him. But she realized that there was time for that later. Right now, she needed to comfort him. Jai needed her.

She took two steps forward again and Jai just moved further back. They did this forward-backward motion until finally Jai had run out of room. There was nowhere he could go now. Shyamita moved in closer, put her arms around him and placed her head on his chest.

At first Jai resisted. He didn't want her to see his vulnerability. He hated being weak.

But then Shyamita nuzzled closer to him and said, 'We don't have to talk about it, Jai. For now, let's just have this moment. Let's just have us.' Saying that she lifted her head to gaze up into his eyes and said, 'Okay?'

For Jai, that was enough. He grabbed her waist, hauled her even closer to himself and crushed her mouth in a soul-searing kiss. It was as though he had been hanging from the cliff for too long and suddenly Shyamita had presented herself as the glimmer of hope. With her by his side, he would make it. He would survive *it*.

The kiss that started off as a hot, hard and deeply passionate soon turned into a slow, languid exploration; their breaths mingling and their souls merging. Shyamita held onto Jai as if he was her lifejacket. Jai never wanted to let go of her.

Gasping for breath, Jai lifted his head and took in a huge gulp of air. And then he threw his head back and started to laugh out loud. Surprised, Shyamita looked up at him only to join him about ten seconds later.

'What the hell have we been doing for the last twelve years, Mithi?' Jai exclaimed, amidst laughter.

'Clearly nothing,' came Shyamita's response.

Eventually the laughter subsided. Their eyes met, and once again Shyamita could feel her breath escaping her lungs in a big whoosh. Jai on his part could feel a stirring deep within and deep down as well. He gently cupped her face with his hands and kissed her lightly on her forehead. Folding her into his embrace again, a soft sigh escaped him. Jai knew there were certain things that he needed to tell her; things she was supposed to know. But tonight, Jairam Nair wanted to be selfish. And he wanted this woman all to himself, without the shadows of his past weighing him down.

The walk to Jai's bedroom was completed in a tangle of limbs and fabric. Jai almost tripped on Shyamita's sari and Shyamita on her part was doing a rather imperfect job of unbuttoning Jai's black kurta before finally giving up and ripping the fabric. She slid off the kurta and finally had Jairam Nair half-naked in front of her. *He was gorgeous!* There was no other word that came to her mind as she ran her hands all across his chest, pinching a nipple and gently teasing the smattering of dark hair that ran down from his sternum all the way down to his rock-hard abs, and waist before disappearing into the folds on his dhoti. When she reached his dhoti, her fingers impatiently untying the knot before his hands stopped her.

'Wait, Mithi. If I'm to be half-naked, you cannot be fully clothed, sweetheart. Where's the justice in that?' he teased her before attacking her sari. Her pleats were the first to fall to the floor. They were then followed by the pallu. He slowly slid it off her left shoulder and down her left arm, until finally the sari was on the floor. In just her red and gold blouse and cream underskirt, she looked utterly beautiful, the rubies, crystals and diamonds sparkling in the moonlight that filtered through the white linen drapes that hung from the floor to ceiling-high windows. It took every ounce of self-control he possessed to not rip every last remaining fabric off her body and bury himself in her.

But Jai knew this had to be special. She was his Mithi after all. Everything about her was special. So he took it slow.

Shyamita blushed crimson as Jai drank in the sight she presented. She had never considered herself to be all that pretty. She thought she was too short and a little too curvy for her own good. In Paris, she was always a little out of place among all the tall, slender women that would strut down the Champs-Élysées. Shyamita had always been comfortable in her long skirts and dresses. The occasional short dress would put her on the receiving end of some major ogling, but nothing like the kind that the Parisian women dealt with every day.

But tonight, with the way Jai was looking at her, she felt beautiful. It was like her very core was on fire. A fire that had been ignited and stoked by only one man – Jairam Nair. It brought out a boldness in her that she never knew she had. One by one, she unfastened the hooks that were on the front of her red and gold blouse. She untied the stringed fabric which held her blouse together from the back. She caught Jai watching her hungrily. He was stumped. She knew she had shocked him. And before her courage could desert her, she slipped out of her blouse and proceeded to untie the underskirt as well. The skirt fell to her feet and she swiftly stepped out of the pool that the fabric had made. Her hands moved to untie her hair when Jai caught her hands and stopped her.

'No. Wait.' And he drank her in once again. She stood there in front of him wearing a crimson strapless lacey bra which just skimmed the top of her breasts, a pair of lacy panties in the same shade of red, rubies and diamonds shimmering in her ears and around her neck, and 6 inch tall crimson peep-toes. Her toenails were painted red and had golden tips. But what made Jai's breath hitch was the rubies and crystals encrusted cummerbund that still encircled Shyamita's waist.

*Oh, man! This woman is a goddess...*he thought. His hands once again encircled her waist. But this time they didn't stay in one place. They explored every inch of her waist. All Shyamita could do was moan and throw her head back. He kissed her at the base of her throat, where he could feel her pulse throbbing frantically. His index finger dipped into her belly button and Shyamita nearly passed out from the sensations. She nearly fell backwards and so Jai scooped her up into his arms. Shyamita's arms went around his neck, her head rested against his shoulder. The best place for her to be – Jai's arms.

He carried her to the large king-sized bed, the cool white satin sheets doing very little to cool down their hot, sweaty bodies. A tangle of arms and legs, it was their mouths which managed to find their way to each other. Jai moaned deep in his throat as Shyamita's tongue forced its way into his mouth. She was under him and wrapped her arms and legs around him and gave way to all the emotions and sensations that pulsated within her every time she was near Jai. With her red heels in the air, Shyamita felt like some kind of sexy siren, the kinds that she'd seen in movies and read about in novels. She kissed him with equal vigor. Her fingers knotted into his hair and her bare thighs grazed against the silken material of his dhoti.

Tearing her mouth away from his in order to breathe, Shyamita moaned, 'Jai', he cupped her breast with one hand. Her nipple peaked through the fabric and she forgot to breathe. His mouth was now making a slow exploratory journey. He planted a soft chaste kiss on the base of her throat. His free hand was much faster than his mouth and slowly skimmed her soft breasts, down the length of her smooth abdomen to her navel and further down till it reached the hem of her panties. His other hand still continued to tease her breast and Shyamita arched back into the mattress, scrunching up the sheets in her hands. She was a jangling bundle of nerves filled with sensations that she had never ever felt before.

'Jai...please...I...' Shyamita was incapable of stringing even two sensible words together.

Jai lifted his head a fraction, just enough to look into her eyes. 'What is it, Mithi?'

'Jai...I...' she stuttered.

'Tell. Me. What. You. Want. Mithi,' he said staccato.

'Jai...I...you,' Shyamita struggled as she felt Jai's fingers touch her through her panties.

'Tell me, Shyamita,' he commanded.

'You,' she breathed and his mouth came crashing down on hers.

The kiss turned slow and tender after the initial onslaught. After kissing her neck, he proceeded further down and on reaching her breast, he moaned, 'Shyamita,' in a deep, throaty voice, before unhooking the front clasp of her bra and revealing her firm breasts. Jai felt as though he had just encountered ambrosia. He dipped his head and took her into his mouth and suckled. And at the same time, his other hand moved her panties to a side and he slid a long finger into her soft, hot folds.

Shyamita's whole world came to a standstill. Nothing mattered. Nothing at all. Except this man - this absolutely gorgeous man, who at this very moment, was wreaking havoc on her body. She arched back and her head dipped further into the mattress.

But now Shyamita couldn't take it any longer. She reached down to where his abdomen touched hers and swiftly untied the knot on his dhoti. Jai smiled against her breast and said, 'Getting impatient are we, love?'

'You have no idea, Jairam Nair,' Shyamita moaned as Jai ripped her panties to shreds. She quickly kicked off her shoes, and now she was gloriously, unabashedly naked except for the jewels glittering in the fading moonlight. And in one quick motion she got up, pushed Jai down onto the mattress and proceeded to divest him of his dhoti and red silk boxers, which earned him a wink of wicked appreciation from her. Jai laughed, a deep guttural laugh, stretched to his bedside bureau and took out a foil packet. He ripped it open, slid on the condom, within seconds pinned Shyamita under him and entered her.

And just as the setting moon and the rising sun cast a ray of magic into his bedroom, Shyamita and Jai came undone in each other's arms.

Shyamita woke up to new surroundings.

Where was she?

Oh! A slow blush began to bloom as she recalled the events of a few hours ago.

Jai! She sighed and stretched languidly on the king-sized bed and reached out to the man who had captured all her dreams in a bottle of stardust and sprinkled it all on her just a few hours ago.

But he wasn't there. Shyamita frowned and sat up to see that the space next to her on the bed was empty. No Jai. But there was a note on his pillow.

Gone out to fetch some breakfast. Be back soon. J.

Shyamita smiled in spite of herself. How perfect could this man be? Not only had he spent the night making mad passionate love to her, not once but twice, now he was out getting breakfast. Shyamita couldn't help it. She sighed again.

She sat up straighter and hugged Jai's pillow, which smelled of his woody cologne and musky aftershave and looked around his bedroom.

White linen drapes hung from the floor to ceiling windows which overlooked a small terrace. In one corner stood small book shelves. A huge walk-in closet dominated the wall opposite a king-sized bed. The other wall had portraits of Jai's favorite authors and their accompanying quotes were written on the whitewashed wall in black and gold embossed paint. There was a small bureau next to the bed which had photographs of his mother and sister. On the far end of the room, right next to the walk-in closet, was the bathroom.

Shyamita slipped out of the covers and got out of bed. The wooden floor warm against her feet, she padded softly to the walk-in closet in search of a towel. She flipped a switch on and several white bulbs were illuminated. On the left-hand side were racks and racks of white shirts, and the typical blues, grays were followed by pastel kurtas by the dozen. Rows of t-shirts were next. On the right-hand side were trousers, chinos, shorts, pajamas and suits. The bottom shelves that ran through both sides were dedicated to shoes. This man's closet and collection of shoes could make even Carrie Bradshaw turn into a green-eyed monster. On the extreme right side of the closet was a single three-level cabinet. The first cabinet was full of perfumes and colognes. The second cabinet had two drawers full of underwear and socks. In the third cabinet, Shyamita found what she was looking for. The softest Turkish towels in various sizes and light pastel colors were neatly stacked together. Shyamita picked up the first one, straightened up, and was just about to flick the light switch off when a thought struck her. Realizing she had nothing to wear, she quickly rummaged through Jai's underwear drawer and picked out a pair of Justice League boxers. From the t-shirts section, she picked up a plain white ganji. Turning off the lights, she shut the door to the closet and padded across to the bathroom.

Rummaging through the bath cabinet, she found spare toothbrushes. She took out one from its packaging and started to brush her teeth. That was when Shyamita saw her reflection in the mirror.

'Oh!' A sigh escaped her lips. Her hair was a tangled mess, her cheeks were flushed. And her eyes looked like the irises had been replaced by stars. She was glowing. And the rubies, diamonds, and crystals still adorning her neck and ears made her sparkle. Despite the fact that her mouth was full of toothpaste right now, Shyamita Bose was sparkling!

11

Fifteen minutes later, Shyamita walked into the living room dressed in Justice League boxers, with the Bat Symbol sitting prettily on her backside, and a white ganji which was so lose, that it looked like an off-shoulder top. She was wearing the bra from last night. Jai had practically shredded her panties.

In the kitchen, she prepared a pot of coffee and made some fresh orange juice from the oranges that were in a fruit basket next to the coffeemaker. In one of the cabinets she found two mugs for coffee and in another she found some biscuits. Placing them all on a large tray, she carried it to the cozy dining table. After placing the tray on the table, she walked over to the bookshelf and began perusing titles, looking for some of Jai's work. She'd only read two out of his seven works. Between the hardbound copies of his books, Shyamita found a thin book of just about hundred-odd pages. It was titled – *Letters and Poems to Mother, by J. L. Nair.*

She pulled out the book and was just about to open it when the front door opened and Jai walked in with two brown bags. Shyamita put the book down next to the LED and walked across to help him.

They put everything on the dining table and finally turned to face each other.

'Hi,' she said shyly.

'Hey!' came his response.

'What time did you wake up?' she asked.

'I barely slept, Mithi,' Jai answered.

'Oh. Why?'

'I was too busy watching you sleep,' he answered and pulled her into his arms. 'Now, it is a good morning,' and proceeded to kiss her softly but passionately. Shyamita's arms circled his neck and she pressed herself into him. Before long they were both gasping for air.

'Well… what do we have here?' he said, taking in her clothes. He put his hands on her waist and turned her around. 'What a spot for the Bat Symbol. I don't think even Nolan could have come up with a better place,' he teased and promptly pinched her on her bottom.

'Jai!' Shyamita whirled around in surprise. Her face had once again turned into a tomato and she couldn't bring herself to look at him.

'What?' he asked in mock innocence.

'Behave, Jairam Nair,' Shyamita said in a voice that was anything but stern.

'Where's the fun in that?' Jai whispered in her ear and a slow tingle spread from Shyamita's neck all the way down her spine to her toes.

She wriggled out of his arms and ran to the other side of the table, as if putting a table between them would stop them from jumping each other's bones.

'Mithi, c'mon…,' he started to walk around the table.

'Jai, stop it,' she said and started moving towards the living room. He didn't stop. So Shyamita screeched and ran. Jai started after her. And soon they were running around the living room, much like they used to chase each other in the school cafeteria, or the chemistry lab, or even in the library. The librarian, Ms Coelho would detain them later for having created a ruckus in a place that, to her, was sacred.

Infectious laughter chimed throughout the living room. At one point, Jai caught up with Shyamita but she threw a cushion at him and sprinted to the other end of the room. Jai started after her again and Shyamita darted towards the dining area. Only this time her left foot hit the leg of the table and she screamed out in pain.

Jai reached her just as she was about to fall. He caught her in time and scooped her up into his arms. Tears were streaming down her cheeks as the pain was almost unbearable.

'Mithi, I'm sorry,' Jai said helplessly. He looked down at her face scrunched up in pain and felt like kicking himself for doing this to her. He was back in that hospital room in Goa, twelve years ago. When he'd entered the hospital room to find so many monitors linked to her, his heart had sunk. He'd cursed himself over and over again for letting their fight carry on for so many days that she'd ended up doing something as reckless as this. He should have gone with her to Goa. None of it would have happened had he been with her.

But nothing had changed. He was just as helpless now as he was then. 'I am so sorry, sweetheart,' he whispered in her ear as he carried her to the couch. He didn't put her down. Instead he sat down with her in his lap. He hugged her tightly and rocked her back and forth.

Eventually, Shyamita's tears stopped. The pain had also reduced down to a dull throbbing.

'Jai, I'm fine now,' she mumbled into his chest. But he continued to rock her.

She wriggled her head up and out of his tight hold and said, 'Jai…'

And that's when he stopped his motion and looked down at her. The concern in his eyes, and the fact that he was still holding her so tightly that at any minute now she would hear her bones cracking, told her just how big a fright she had given him. She immediately realized that he was thinking about her drowning accident in Goa. She remembered how glad she had been when she had opened her eyes and found Jai asleep in a chair beside the bed. She'd forgotten all about their fight and had just taken in the sight of him. When he'd woken up, what had followed was a bout of reassurances that she was absolutely fine. And she had to do that again now.

She managed to extricate a hand out of his tight hold and cupped his face. 'I am fine, Jai,' she insisted. 'You can put me down.'

But Jai shook his head.

'No?' she asked.

He shook his head again.

'But I'm fine, darling,' she smiled.

'You sure?' came his query, soft and unsure.

'Yes, I'm fine,' she assured him gently.

'Okay. But I am not putting you down,' he said firmly and stood up with her in his arms.

'Arre!' was all she could say because the look he gave her told her that he was in no mood to argue.

Shyamita put her index finger on her lips and winked at him. He smiled weakly and walked to the dining table. He put her on the table and got down on one knee to have a look at her ankle. His large hand easily encircled her slender ankle. Shyamita grimaced at the contact. It still hurt, even after so many years.

A long thin scar stretched from mid-calf to her ankle. Jai traced the scar with his index finger. This time Shyamita's breath hitched, not in pain, but because of the sensations that one touch sent through her body. He looked up at her and asked, 'Does it still hurt?"

'Only when I put pressure on it,' she told him in an assuring tone.

'I am sorry, Mithi,' he said again.

'It's not your fault, Jai. I should be more careful,' she replied, trying to pacify him.

'No. It is my fault. I shouldn't have chased you like that,' he was still apologetic.

'Jairam Nair, listen to me,' she said sternly. 'It is NOT your fault. And I refuse to let you wallow in guilt all day when we can actually have a wonderful day together,' she ended, her voice firm but indulgent.

Jai smiled. He bent his head down and kissed her ankle. This was all too much for Shyamita to bear. She bent down, grabbed his shoulders and pulled him up. Tears welled in her eyes again. She entwined her fingers at the back of his neck, pulled him down to her and kissed him deeply. When she lifted her mouth from his, a tear trickled down her cheek. Jai lightly brushed it away with his thumb-pad and kissed her on her forehead.

'Mithi,' he asked her as he sat down on a chair, 'tell me about your accident.'

'Jai…it was a really long time ago,' she said.

'So what?' he countered. 'I'd like to know. Please.'

And Shyamita obviously couldn't refuse now.

She took a deep breath and began, 'On my twentieth birthday, I went out with my friends for dinner. By the end of the night, we were all pretty wasted. So I decided to stay over at my friend's place. One of my friends had brought his father's cell phone. So I used it to call Baba and tell him that it was too late for me to come home and that he should not stay up. We had just finished having our softie ice creams at Pasteurs. You remember that café we had gone to when you, Karan, and Geet had come to Pune before our board exams?' Jai nodded, and she continued, 'Baba wasn't answering his cell phone. So I decided to text him. I was so engrossed in texting that I didn't hear the sound of an approaching car before it was too late. The car hit me and I fell into a ditch.' Shyamita shuddered at the memory. Her whole world had come crashing down. She had never been able to dance after that night.

'I broke my ankle bone and the bone of my heel cracked,' she closed her eyes as she said those words, the pain still etched on her face. 'I still have a hairline fracture,' she ended.

Jai watched the emotions playing out on Shyamita's face. He'd known that she'd met with an accident some years ago. Geet had told Karan and he had told Jai. But he didn't know the extent of Shyamita's injuries until now.

'So that's why you gave up dancing.'

'Yes, I had to. But I have no regrets, Jai,' she said. 'After the accident, I took nearly eight months to recover fully. By then, I made up my mind about pursuing art. After Baba retired from the Army, he and Ma decided to settle in Pune. It had been his last posting and they had come to love the city. So I joined Abhinav Kala Mandir, where I studied for about a year. I then travelled across India, lived in some of the most remote villages and immersed myself in the art and culture of our country. It was around this time that

Paris happened. I went on an art scholarship and fell madly in love with the city.'

'I've always wanted to be an artist, Jai, you know that. Granted, initially, it was a little difficult with Ma and Baba constantly worrying about whether or not I would ever be able to dance again. Today, however, they are proud of what I have achieved. It hasn't been an easy journey, I have to admit. But I'm glad I have been able to do so much.'

As he listened to the way she spoke so emphatically about her achievements, Jai realized that she wasn't the kind of woman who needed a man's protection. She was her own person. She was the kind of woman you wanted to share everything with. She was an equal. And he admired that about her. She was different. And around her, he felt different. He felt alive for the first time in twelve years.

'At least, you can dance with me, Mithi,' he teased.

'A girl can always dream, Jai,' she teased back.

Breakfast was a simple affair; sandwiches, egg-white omelets and hash-browns – all from a nearby café. Shyamita was still sitting on the table and her foot was resting on Jai's thigh. He was as stubborn as a raging bull.

While sipping coffee, which had to be reheated, Jai said, 'Do you know what I was thinking while I watched you sleep?'

Shyamita shook her head.

'I was thinking...*if I could wake up to your face every morning, for the rest of my life I'd want for nothing.*'

Shyamita was speechless. Her coffee mug forgotten in her hands, she just stared at Jai.

Jairam Nair is reciting poetry to me...her heart was dancing happily and her brain had gone all fuzzy and woolly. All manner of coherent thought had receded to the very back of her head. She just felt warm and gooey all over.

Her foot that was resting on Jai's lap had other plans. She wriggled her toes and dug them into the inside of his thigh. She could see desire flaring in Jai's eyes. She could also feel his tightness underneath the thin material of his cotton chinos. Shyamita set her coffee mug aside and slid closer to Jai. She moved her left leg onto the other side of the chair and brought her right leg up. And she smiled! Jai was trapped.

And it seemed her prisoner didn't mind being trapped at all. He ran his hands up her bare calves, skimmed over knees and then slowly travelled upwards. He stopped at her upper thighs and began to massage them through her boxer shorts. He inched closer and closer to her womanhood, and Shyamita thought she would explode. Finally, he slid his hand underneath the hem of her boxers and touched her intimately. Shyamita's head fell back and she had to support herself by placing her elbows on the table. Jai got up from his chair and kicked it all the way back to the wall.

His cell phone began to ring but he silenced it and flung it onto the couch in the living room. He made quick work of her boxers, shucked off his chinos and briefs and plunged into her. In a matter of minutes, they were good and lost.

'Geet!' Shyamita screamed and leapt up from the floor, having collapsed onto it with Jai after making love in the most primitive of ways imaginable. *Sex on the table!* Sigh.

Jai watched Shyamita as she made a dash for clothes and in the process spilled coffee, and almost broke a mug. She was about to trip again when Jai bolted into action and caught hold of her.

'Shyamita! Relax,' he said, trying his best not to laugh as she tried to calm down.

She looked at him with panic in her eyes. 'Geet…Jai, she's going to kill me.'

'Oh, please. That she-hulk is going to be busy looking into the mirror. It won't even dawn on her that you're not there,' he added for good measure, but only to be punched on his chest.

'Shut up, Jai,' she said. 'We have to go. She'll be frantic with worry,' she said as she tried to once again wriggle out of Jai's arms. This was becoming routine now.

'Mithi, she won't be worried. I spoke to Karan this morning when I was out picking up breakfast,' he told her. 'I asked him to hold the fort and wrestle the tornado.'

Shyamita still wasn't convinced.

Jai soldiered on. 'Mithi, there's no wedding-related event happening today. Geet and Karan are going to be at the gurdwara all evening for paath.'

'I think I should call Geet,' Shyamita was rambling, barely listening to what Jai was saying.

Jai sighed and walked over to the couch and retrieved his cell phone. He handed it to Shyamita who dialed Geet's number frantically. Geet picked up on the second ring.

'Jairam Nair! Where the bloody hell are you? Where is Shyamita? Where is she? I want to speak to her. Give her the phone now. Oh, you're in such a lot of trouble, Nair! You have no idea. I am going to skin you alive. I am…'

'Geet!' Shyamita cut into her tirade. Geet had been shouting so loudly that despite the fact that Shyamita had not turned on the speakerphone, Jai had heard every word.

'Geet, I'm here. I'm fine,' she barely managed before Geet launched at her.

'How can you be so irresponsible, Shyamita Bose? Do you have any idea how worried I've been? I was just going to call Karan and tell him to come and pick you up from that moron's house.'

'Geet, will you just relax? I'm fine. I was exhausted last night, and so slept until late,' said Shyamita, lying through her teeth.

'Late? LATE???' Geet's voice had reached supersonic mode. Pretty soon only bats would be able to hear her. 'It is two-thirty in the afternoon. You call that late?' she screeched.

Shyamita's eyes widened when she heard the time. Two-thirty! How could she have been so irresponsible? Geet was right.

Jai saw the emotions playing out on Shyamita's face and immediately knew that Geet was getting to her. He snatched the phone from Shyamita and muttered, 'Chadda, stop behaving like a fire-breathing dragon. I'll have her home after dinner,' and he ended the call before he could hear anymore of Geet's supersonic threats.

At the Chadda House, on the second floor, a loud bang was heard from inside the bride-to-be's room as she flung her phone at the wall.

'So what do you want to do?' Jai asked sheepishly.

Shyamita, whose jaw had almost hit the floor at the way Jai had just casually hung up on Geet could only manage a squeaky, 'Huh?'

'I asked, what do you want to do?' he repeated his question.

'Oh,' she said, coming back to reality, 'Umm...I don't know, Jai.'

Beginning to get a little annoyed, 'Mithi, I just told you Geet and Karan are going to be busy all evening. C'mon!'

Shyamita looked up at Jai apologetically, 'You're right. I'm sorry,' and, then smiling, she said, 'So, what do you have in mind?'

Jai grinned. 'I think a shower is in order. What say you?'

It was a good hour later that Jai and Shyamita stepped out of the house. The shower took a little longer than they had anticipated. But Jai blamed Shyamita for being a distraction and she blamed him for being...well, for being him.

Shyamita was dressed in a pale green summer dress with small white flowers and plain white sneakers, both of which she had found in Naina's closet. She wore the same bra from the previous night and since there was no way she could salvage her panties, she was wearing a brand new pair of white boxers. Her hair was left to hang loose around her shoulders. And in spite of the fact that she wasn't wearing any make-up, Jai thought he had never seen a more beautiful woman in his life.

Dressed in beige cargo shorts, a plain white polo t-shirt under a shirt with white and blue checks, and dark blue moccasins, he looked good enough to eat, Shyamita thought as Jai fastened his helmet in the garage. She was wearing a yellow helmet that was thankfully not gigantic like Jai's. Rather it was a cute, girly one. She wondered whose it was and was about to ask Jai when he said, 'I bought this for Naina when she was visiting. So it's pretty new.'

The first stop they made was at a nearby restaurant that was famous for local delicacies. Their breakfast had been digested long ago owing to two very vigorous sessions of lovemaking. So they wolfed down a plate of missal paav, a spicy curry of sprouts topped with crispy potato shreds, onions, lemon and coriander, served with delicious, toasted bread. Next on the menu was roasted, grilled Pomfret. Grilled to perfection, the fish literally sang to the Bengali in Shyamita. For dessert they shared hot gulab jamuns and phirni. Jai couldn't help but smile at the way Shyamita attacked her food. But given the fact that he had completely tired her out a couple of hours ago, he couldn't blame her. As he watched her demolish a gulab jamun he recalled the agony she had been in when her foot had hit the chair. He still felt guilty for having pushed her to scamper across to the dining area like that. He had felt completely helpless and useless when she was writhing in pain.

Jai didn't want to put much into his thoughts. But he knew that sooner or later he would have to come face-to-face with his feelings for her. For now, though, he was just happy he had her to himself.

It was close to five o'clock when they stepped out of the restaurant. 'Where to now, Ms Bose?' Jai asked as he started his bike.

Shyamita's reply was instant and predictable. 'Marine Drive. Sunset.'

Mumbai's relentless traffic and endless traffic jams ensured that they reached Marine Drive half an hour later, when it shouldn't have taken them more than ten minutes. But that was really the charm of the city, Shyamita thought as she got off the motorcycle. Despite its humid weather and deplorable traffic conditions, it never failed to surprise you at every turn. The city had given her Jai. And for that one reason alone, she would be eternally grateful. She didn't know where she and Jai were headed. She didn't know what was going to happen to them three days from now when the wedding functions and ceremonies were over. She was leaving for Pune the following Monday and for Paris two weeks later. She didn't even know Jai's plans.

But she didn't want to overanalyse right now. For once, she wanted to live in the moment.

The rocks were warm and wet as Jai and Shyamita made their way to their favorite spot, shoes in hand. Once there, they sat down and sipped coconut water which Jai had bought from a vendor. In front of them lay miles and miles of water which had now turned into a deep shade of orange and the sky painted in marvelous hues of red, orange, and yellow – a breathtaking sight to behold.

'It's so beautiful,' Shyamita exclaimed as she laid her head on Jai's shoulder.

'Hmm…I agree,' he said and laid his head on hers. 'An artist's paradise.'

'Yes,' came her response as she closed her eyes and breathed in the warm sultry air that had mingled with the saltiness of the sea.

'You should recreate this scene on your canvas, Mithi,' Jai said after a while.

Shyamita simply smiled, as she tried to brush her hair back from her face. Jai caught her hand and she looked at him, a question in her eyes.

'What?' he asked innocently.

'I'm getting blinded here, Jai. You mind letting go of my hand?' her voice firm, but indulgent all the same.

His hand still in hers, he leaned closer to her and whispered in her ear, 'It seems your hair has suddenly developed a mind of its own and has chosen to dance with the winds of the sea. I like the way it's dancing. I think this view is meant for an artist's canvas.'

Shyamita's breath hitched and she blushed scarlet for the umpteenth time in less than twenty-four hours. Like warm honey poured over sinful dark chocolate, his voice could probably melt even glaciers, Shyamita thought.

She shivered as Jai blew softly into her ear. He released her hand, cupped her face and drew her mouth to his.

They had to kiss again. By the sea. *By their mistletoe.*

The waves crashed against the rocks and within no time, Jai and Shyamita were drenched from head to toe. The sun had almost disappeared into the water. The sea was now a deep shade of orange and vermillion, and in the distance one could see the white glimmer of the rising moon. It was a sight to behold indeed. As though in cahoots with the sun and moon, the clouds seemed to have disappeared altogether and the sky played host to two lovers who had only these two minutes of togetherness before one set and the other rose to its brightest.

Shyamita and Jai witnessed this beautiful scene from their place on the rocks. *Are we like the sun and moon? Would we have a happy ending? Or would they also have just this one day together?*

The piercing sound of a whistle interrupted Shyamita's thoughts. Jai, who was sleeping against her shoulder, jerked upright upon hearing the sound.

'What...what is it?' he asked.

Before she could answer, a pot-bellied hawaldar with a hennaed moustache, dressed in his khakis, with a long bamboo cane in his hand and a sly grin on his face, walked up to where they were sitting. Behind him Shyamita could see young couples running helter-skelter.

The hawaldar stood right in front of them and grinned. He then banged his cane against the rocks next to Jai and said in Marathi, 'Well well well...what have we here? Sirjee, this is a public beach. And you and,' he looked at Shyamita in her wet clothes and grinned slyly again, 'madamjee are sitting like this...'

Jai shot up to his feet and stood between the hawaldar and Shyamita. He was furious. Barely controlling his temper, he said in a low but menacing voice, 'I think it'd be best if you spoke and looked at me directly.'

The hawaldar who had taken a step back upon seeing Jai's towering height, cleared his throat, all his bravado gone, and said, 'Sirjee, I am only cautioning you and your wife. There are other cops who are not as understanding as me, Sirjee.'

'My wife and I will keep that in mind,' Jai said in a voice that brooked no nonsense. 'Will that be all?' he asked the hawaldar. The poor man nodded and stepped aside to make way for them.

Shyamita, who had frozen when the cop had referred to her as Jai's wife, was hauled to her feet by him.

'Let's go, Mithi,' said Jai, and helped her up the rocks and back to the top.

The hawaldar, who had also reached the top, tipped his cap at Jai and said, 'Goodnight to you and your Mrs, Sirjee,' and walked away.

12

All her life Shyamita had dreamed of being Jai's wife. She had fallen in love with him way back when they were in sixth grade. He had been the boy who had beaten up a classmate, Varad, for trying to look up her skirt. Jai had been taken to the principal's office and suspended for a week, but that didn't stop Shyamita from falling in love with him. Her fairytale had started taking shape when she was only twelve. Since then, the two of them had been inseparable. Their English teacher Ms Jacinta would always say that they were joined at the hip. And Shyamita would revel in that.

So today, when the hawaldar had referred to her as Jai's wife, she was shocked yes, but secretly, she was thrilled. Her eyes had turned into giant saucers and she was sure her cheeks looked like they had been smeared with beetroot.

The two of them made their way to where Jai had parked his motorcycle with Jai still holding Shyamita's hand. Just as they reached his motorcycle, Jai's cell phone began to ring. He dug it out of his pocket, 'It's Karan,' he told Shyamita, and put the call on speakerphone.

'Hey!' he said a little too brightly, as he put his arm around Shyamita's shoulder and pulled her to his side.

'Umm…Hi, Jai.' Karan's reaction was just what Jai had been hoping for.

'What's happening, bro?' Shyamita knew Jai was trying to rile up Geet, just in case she was on the other side with Karan.

'Err...nothing much. We are at the gurdwara,' Karan replied in a low whisper.

'Awesome!' *Too bright, Jairam Nair!* Shyamita looked up at him, with a warning in her eyes. But Jai only winked at her and pulled her closer, kissing the top of her head.

'Jai, listen up,' Karan continued, 'we are going to be pulling an all-nighter here at the gurdwara. Geet's grandmother has organized an all-night paath,' his voice growing softer with every word.

'Okay…,' now Jai was confused.

'Yes,' said Karan.

'Umm…this is all you wanted to say? Is this why you called?' Jai asked, with growing irritation.

'No, you idiot!' Karan hissed. 'I called to say that you and Shyamita can have another night out together.'

Now it was Jai's turn to have eyes as wide as saucers.

'Err… Karan, you know what you're saying right? Where's Geet?' Jai had to ask.

'She's inside. I just stepped out saying I've to make a work-related call,' came Karan's reply.

Shyamita and Jai could only stare at each other.

'Okay, I've to go now,' Karan's voice came back, 'You guys have a good time. Bye!' and the call ended.

They were still speechless. *What had just happened?*

Finally, it was Jai who broke the silence by saying, 'You see! This is what friends do. Unlike your friend, who only opens her mouth to threaten others with bodily harm.'

Shyamita had to laugh at that.

❧❧

As Karan climbed the steps to the gurdwara, he knew he would be in a lot of trouble with Geet if she ever found out what he had done. She'd probably kill him. But Karan also knew that this had to be done. Jai and Shyamita needed to spend more time together to realize that they could not live without each other.

For years, he'd seen Jai go out with woman after woman, but not one had lasted more than a couple of months. Yesterday, he'd seen how Jai couldn't stop staring at Shyamita when she had walked into the garden. He'd also noticed his friend's annoyance and the flash of temper in his eyes when he had complimented Shyamita.

Karan knew Jai was in love. Now if only that idiot would realize it and not let Shyamita get away again!

❧❧

They decided to go back to Jai's home and order in. But first, Shyamita needed to go to Geet's house and pick up clothes. More importantly, she needed to pick up fresh underwear. Jai waited downstairs and made a few calls while Shyamita went up to her room to pick up her stuff. His agent had been calling him all day, but he had put her on his 'ignore list'. Finally the woman had given up on calling him, and sent him a barrage of text messages instead. The next instalment of his book was due. He had six book-signing tours coming up. A television reporter wanted to interview him on his latest book making it to the *New York Times* Bestsellers list.

'Hi, Anita,' he tried to sound as if he had no idea his agent had been trying to reach him frantically all day.

'Jai! Where the hell are you? I've been trying to reach you all bloody day,' Anita Rodriguez barked into the phone.

'You have?' Jai replied, all innocent.

'Don't get cute with me. You know I have. You put me on that bloody 'ignore list',' she said in a much calmer voice. But Jai knew this could very well be the lull before the storm.

'Okay, okay. I'm sorry,' he said in a much more placating tone. 'Tell me what's on the immediate agenda?'

'Shall I order pizza?' Jai asked Shyamita as soon as he shut the front door behind them.

'Err...yeah, okay,' she told him hesitantly and without making any eye contact with him, she walked over to the couch, straightened the cushions, and placed her overnight bag on the floor. She then walked to the dining table and poured herself a glass of water from the jug.

She had been silent all throughout the short ride from Geet's house. Something was up. Jai intended to find out what it was.

He walked over to the dining table, took the empty glass from Shyamita's hand and placed it on the table. She still wasn't looking at him. Instead, she kept her eyes on the glass.

He caught her chin and tried to make her look at him, but she looked down at her feet instead. Exasperated he asked, 'Mithi, what is it?'

She didn't answer.

'Are you mad at me for the way I spoke to Geet?' he asked.

She shook her head.

'Okay. Are you mad at me for bringing you here?'

She shook her head.

'Okay. Are you mad at me…?'

'I am not mad at you, Jai,' she said in a low voice.

'Then what is it?'

'I...er...I don't want you to think I do this often,' she said in the same low voice.

'Do what?' Jai was totally confused now.

'This.'

'What is 'this'?' she was confusing him even more.

Finally, she looked up at him and said, 'I don't sleep around, Jairam Nair.'

Okay, now the confusion had turned into befuddlement. 'Who says you're sleeping around?'

'Nobody said that. I just want you to know that I don't sleep around,' her voice was firm once again.

'Mithi, where is all this coming from?' It was like she had dropped a bomb on him and he just didn't know what to make of it.

'I'm just telling you,' she added in a firm voice, yet again.

His fingers were still holding her chin in place. He cupped her face with both his hands and, in a very calm and composed voice, said to her, 'Shyamita Bose, not even for one second did I think that you sleep around.' He took a deep breath and went on, 'I don't know what brought this ridiculous notion into your head. I, for one, have never thought of you in such a way, and I'll probably punch anybody who thinks that way about you.'

He kissed her on her forehead and drew her into his embrace. *Home* couldn't have been a better place than this.

They stood there, in his dining room, for god alone knows how long. Finally, in a teasing voice Jai asked Shyamita, 'so pizza, or is mademoiselle going to cook?'

Shyamita smiled into his shoulder, raised her head and looked into his eyes. She saw the teasing glint in his eyes.

'Why monsieur, prepare to lick your fingers clean,' she challenged him.

13

After six rotis, a delicious cashew-based mushroom and peas gravy, mixed vegetable jalfrezi, steamed basmati rice, and apple-biscuit crisp for dessert, Jairam Nair lay sprawled on the couch in the living room. And yes, he did end up licking his fingers clean.

Shyamita sat on the other end of the couch and picked up the book she had abandoned in the morning. But no sooner did she open the book to start reading than she heard a soft rumbling sound coming from Jai. The man had fallen asleep. Right there on his couch; all the day's activities finally catching up with him.

She studied him just like she used to when they were kids in school. Jai would sit on the bench next to her and would sleep in the Geography period. Shyamita, instead of focusing on the political map of India, would study and observe Jai.

Now, as she sat next to him on the couch, she studied him even more intently. She drank him in. His face wasn't that of a conventional south Indian. High cheekbones which were now peppered with a light beard, a square chin with a deep cleft, a long, yet slightly crooked nose that Shyamita had broken accidentally in school during the physical education period, eyes that had unusually thick lashes. His hair which had a few grey peppering the black was styled in such a way that it was long in the front, covering his forehead, and long enough in the back for him to tie a ponytail. She liked that ponytail; it gave him a certain flair.

Setting the book aside, she picked up her overnight bag and laid it gently on the table. Unzipping it, she took out her pencils-kit, her sketchpad, and a small piece of cloth. As a last-minute decision before leaving her room in Geet's house, she had stuffed both the items in her bag. Zipping up her bag, she placed it back next to the couch and walked over to the loveseat on the other end of the living room. She moved the seat, which, thankfully, was light enough despite its rosewood make, to a more advantageous position. She dimmed the lights in the living room so that Jai's sleeping face was illuminated in a way that brought out his innocence. For she truly believed, especially after last night, that there still was a part of Jai that hadn't grown up. He had an innocence about him that was absolutely precious. And it was this innocence that Shyamita wanted to capture.

She took out two sharpened charcoal pencils, a charcoal crayon, an eraser, and two watercolor brushes from her kit and laid them out on the small piece of cloth. She then brought from the kitchen a small glass filled with water. She sat on the loveseat, settled her sketchpad on her thighs and began to make the preliminary contour lines suggesting Jai's facial structure, his hair, as well as the texture of his checked shirt. To highlight his hair she used an HB charcoal pencil. She gently rolled the lead tip across the surface of the paper between the contour lines. This she did in order to highlight his long and wavy hair. With 3B pencils and vine charcoal she darkened the contours of his facial structure, highlighting his strong jaw-line. She used the vine charcoal to emphasize his deep cleft. With water-color brushes she softened the shadows, and with an HB pencil produced a sharper contrast. She then darkened the checks on the collar of his shirt and lightly highlighted his broad shoulders. Next, she worked on the shadows with a 3B pencil.

After some more shading along the contour lines, Shyamita put down her pencil and admired the portrait. In her mind, she was sure she had not done justice to Jai and his…well, for lack of a better word, beauty. In Paris, she had thought of sketching him from memory many times. But the thought itself was too painful for her and so she would abandon the portrait midway.

Once, Mia had walked in on her discarding another abandoned canvas and said, 'You don't need to keep doing this to yourself, Shyamita. Why can't you just get over him already?' she asked in a voice that was full of concern.

Shyamita had laughed it off by saying as nonchalantly as she could, 'Over whom, Mia? C'mon. I'm hungry. Let's go down to Pierre's Café.'

Mia sighed in an all-knowing manner, but complied with Shyamita's request instead of pushing her.

Shyamita got up from her seat and walked over to where Jai was still sleeping; now snoring.

Yikes! He snores.

She set her sketchpad and pencils on the small table beside the couch and settled next to him. She pushed back the hair from his eyes. Such a beautiful specimen this man was. She couldn't get enough of him. Snuggling closer to him, she lay her head on his shoulder and closed her eyes.

As if sensing her nearness, Jai wrapped his arms around her and pulled her closer to him. And once again Shyamita Bose spent the night wrapped tightly in Jairam Nair's arms. But the good thing was, she didn't want to be any place else.

Someone was crying. A helpless sort of weeping. And then came the screams. Shyamita's eyes shot open. It was Jai. He was crying. At some point in the night he had fallen on the floor and was now crying in his sleep. He was thrashing about.

Shyamita quickly slid off the couch and sat next to him on the floor. But she felt helpless. She didn't know what to do. She could see tears clogging his eyelashes and his screams had now turned into wretched sobs. *What was happening? What was he dreaming about?*

But she did not have time to ponder over these questions, because Jai started talking in his sleep.

'Leave her alone,' he sobbed. 'Don't touch her.'

Who was he talking to?

'Don't you dare lay a finger on her!' Jai's soft sob turned into a menacing warning now.

But then, he started sobbing again, this time the tears escaping his shut eyes. Shyamita had never felt so helpless in her life. She gently laid a soothing hand on Jai's forehead, urging him to quieten down and sleep more peacefully. She lay down next to him and whispered softly into his ear, 'It's okay, Jai. I'm right here. It's okay, baby. Go back to sleep.'

She laid her head on his chest and placed her hand on his heart. 'I'm right here, baby. I'm not going anywhere. Hush now, go back to sleep.'

Finally, the sobbing subsided. Shyamita gently wiped the tears from his face, kissed him on both his cheeks before placing a soft kiss on his lips. He stirred then, his eyes opening a fraction.

'I...,' he started to say, but his voice cracked.

'Shh...go back to sleep, love. I'm right here,' she said and settled herself on his chest again. Jai tensed for a moment, then took in a deep breath and slipped into a dreamless sleep.

Why is it so cold? And where is my pillow? Hang on, am I on the floor? Why am I on the floor?

The questions addled Jai's groggy stupor. Slowly opening his eyes to the harsh sunlight that was now generously pouring in from the curtains they had forgotten to draw last night, he took in his surroundings. Okay, so he'd slept on the floor. Not a new thing considering how his childhood had been.

He tried to sit up and that was when he noticed Shyamita's leg across his pelvis. The skirt of her dress had ridden up and he could see the boxers she was wearing. Something very primitive stirred within him when he saw his boxers on her. Her hands were on either side of her head, in a very dancer-like pose. He followed the rhythmic rise and fall of breasts as she breathed. The stirring was now swiftly turning into a tightening. Gently lifting her leg, he extricated himself, and stretched out all the kinks and aching muscles in his body. Brushing back the hair from her face, he kissed her lightly on her cheek. She mumbled something in her sleep and pulled her knees all the way up to her chin. Smiling softly at the angelic picture she presented, he kissed her once again on her cheek and got up from the floor, his back screaming in protest and walked to the kitchen.

Ten minutes later, he walked over to the main door and gently unlocked the door so as to not wake up Sleeping Beauty. He stretched once again in the foyer, rode the elevator down to the lobby and finally stepped out into the morning sun. There was an Archies' gallery just a short walk from Belvedere Tower. On his way to the store, he bumped into his neighbor who was walking his Great Dane.

'How is it going, Mr Sheikh?'

'All good, Jai. What is new with you?' the good man enquired.

'Nothing much. A friend of mine is getting married. So I've just been busy with all the preparations,' Jai supplied, smiling.

'Is that all?' the old man asked, in a teasing manner.

Jai frowned. 'Err...yes, Mr Sheikh. That is all.' And then as if suspecting something, he asked, 'Why?'

The old man shook his head lightly. 'Nothing, nothing. You just seem to be in an unusually good mood this morning,' he laughed and continued with his morning walk.

Jai stared at the old man for a few seconds before heading to the store.

She was still sleeping when Jai walked back into the living room. He closed the main door behind him and sat down right next to Shyamita on the floor. He brushed her hair away from her face and took in her sleeping form. 'You're beautiful, Shyamita Bose,' he said in a husky whisper. She stirred but did not wake up. In her sleep, she moved towards him and he laid her head in his lap. Jai placed the coffee mug on the small table beside the couch and that is when he saw her sketchpad, with the pencils and charcoal strewn across the paper.

Carefully, he pulled the pad from below the scattered stationery. He lifted open the front cover and what he saw stunned him completely. It was a sketch of a young boy playing with his dog on a cobbled street. Behind them, stood a horse-drawn carriage from which a woman was in the process of disembarking. Two of the lamp-posts outside the bakery had broken glass, and atop one perched two sparrows. The detailing took Jai's breath away. The scene looked right out of a fairytale. The next sketch was of a pregnant woman. She was naked, with her lustrous long hair flowing down one side and a book face-down in her lap. She was sitting on a chintz loveseat and her eyes were closed, as if asleep. According to Jai the most poignant aspect of the scene was the way the woman had placed both her hands protectively over her burgeoning stomach. Nothing spelt the joy and anticipation of motherhood more than the way the fingers were splayed across her stomach.

As Shyamita snuggled closer and got more comfortable, Jai pored through all her sketches. There were scenes of children playing in the streets, a proposal at the Eiffel Tower, a boulangerie on the Champs-Élysées, an old couple huddled together in a park on a cold winter night, a father and daughter walking down a crowded road with the focus on how tightly the girl was clasping her father's hands. And then, Jai came across an all-too-familiar face and setting.

When did she sketch me… he wondered.

He traced the lines and contours of his sketch with his fingers. The paper felt rough beneath his exploring fingertips. He had always known he was good looking. Karan had always accused him of being an arrogant ass about it. But not until that moment did he genuinely believe that he was truly fine. Shyamita had sketched him so beautifully and so perfectly. She had even drawn the small jagged scar on his left cheek correctly. His thoughts moved dangerously close to how he had got that scar. But he pushed himself past them and was just about to close his sketchpad when Shyamita stirred.

Eyes barely open, she lifted her head from his lap and looked up at him.

'Good morning, sweetheart,' he said, his voice a husky whisper.

'Good morning,' she returned shyly, pushing the hair away from her face. It was then she noticed her sketchpad in Jai's hands. She quickly got to her feet and tried to snatch the pad from him. But he didn't let go. She tried again. No luck.

'Relax, Mithi. I am not going to steal it,' he said, smiling up at her from his position on the floor.

'Jai, did you see…' she could not complete her question; her face was now possibly brighter than a tomato.

'Did I see what?' he queried, although he knew very well what she was trying to ask him.

'Did you...err...nothing,' she said quickly and once again tried to snatch the sketchpad from his hands.

Jai caught her wrist and pulled her onto his lap, setting the sketchpad on the floor. He opened the cover and turned over the pages to his sketch.

Shyamita screwed her eyes shut.

'Open your eyes, Mithi,' he said softly.

She didn't.

'Please,' he said softly again.

Slowly opening her eyes, she looked at her sketchpad and then looked up at Jai. He was looking down at her, his eyes awash with an emotion she hadn't seen before. She smiled hesitantly, and said, 'I'm sorry. I shouldn't have sketched you like that without your permission.'

'You know, Mithi, if I was an artist, I'd draw you like Leonardo DiCaprio draws Kate Winslet in *Titanic*. Only difference would be you'd be wearing just the Batman Boxers,' he teased her and Shyamita burst out laughing.

He kissed her on her forehead. And in her lap, he placed a small Archies' bag.

'What is this?' she looked up at him.

'Open it, Mithi,' he said softly.

Shyamita ripped open the bag excitedly. Inside was a small cardboard box. Confused, she frowned up at Jai. He simply gestured toward the box and mouthed, 'Open it.' She opened the box and inside, between bubble wrap, sat two tiny yellow mugs, their handles intertwined.

'This is how we are, Mithi. Intertwined. Connected. Always,' his voice was heavy with emotion.

Shyamita looked up at him, but found that once again, she was unable to articulate a response. 'Jai, I…' she started to say but then his mouth came down on hers.

It was the kind of kiss that would make a woman's head turn into candyfloss. It was also the kind of kiss that could make a dormant volcano suddenly active. Sweet and gentle, explosive and passionate... He buried his fingers into her hair and brought her head closer to his, his tongue began an exploration of her mouth, snaking in and out. Shyamita arched her back and pressed her breasts into his chest.

For now, *this was all that mattered*, she said to herself. Everything else came later. Jai came first.

Cradling his head in her hands she pressed a kiss on the top of his head as he began to undo the buttons on her dress. Softly, she whispered, 'I'm all yours, Jai,' and in the same breath also said, 'I won't let anybody hurt you.'

She was lying on top of him; the two of them bathed in sweat and reveling in the aftermath of what had just transported them to the stars and back. 'Thank you,' Jai said in a voice that was so low Shyamita could barely hear him.

'Hmm?' she murmured softly, 'What are you thanking me for, Jai?' She placed the flat of her palms on his chest and raised her torso up so that she could look into his eyes. When he didn't answer, she asked again, 'Jai, why are you thanking me?'

He looked at her then, their eyes locking, and for the longest time Shyamita thought he wasn't going to answer her. His expression was somber, as if he was in deep thought. Finally, he cleared his throat before saying, 'Shyamita, I think we should go to Geet's.'

And Shyamita's face fell.

'What did the two of you do…? Did you stay over at his place both nights…? Where did you sleep? Oh, my god! Did you two do *it*?'

Shyamita wanted to throw something at Geet. From the second Shyamita had stepped into the living room of her house, Geet had been at her throat. She had followed her up to her room, shooting a zillion questions at her. It had not even registered with her that her friend was in no mood to talk.

The way Jai had dismissed her had been so sudden, it had taken her aback completely. After two fantasy-like nights with him, the way he had changed in the short span of thirty minutes had shaken Shyamita to her very core. Rather than dropping her to Geet's place on his motorcycle, Jai had driven his Volvo XC60. The fifteen-minute drive had been completed in less than six minutes. When they reached Geet's he did not even get out of the car and help Shyamita out. Instead he sat stiffly in his seat, and the moment she shut the door, he muttered a curt 'see you later' and drove away.

Right now, Shyamita was hurting. And she really did not want to answer any of Geet's questions.

She sat down on the bed, dumping her overnight bag on the floor. Head bent down, she sat there staring at her folded hands in her lap. She felt defeated. She felt as if all the life had been sucked right out of her.

And she had questions of her own swimming inside her head. *What had brought on the sudden change in him? Why had he thanked her in the first place? And more importantly, what was he not telling her?*

But Geet's voice was reaching supersonic levels. Any minute now the windows in her room would shatter. 'Geet!' she almost screamed, stomping her foot loudly on the floor and finally breaking her silence.

The other girl was momentarily stunned by her friend's rather uncharacteristic response. In all the years that she had known Shyamita, Geet had never seen her throw any kind of tantrum.

'Shyamu,' she began in a placating voice but only to be cut short by Shyamita.

'Geet, can you please leave me alone for a while?' she beseeched her friend in a voice that almost betrayed her. Tears were already pooling in her eyes and threatening to flow down, so Shyamita kept her head bent, not wanting her friend to see her in such a state.

But Geet knew her friend too well. She knew Shyamita was upset and she wanted to know why. But she also knew better than to push her. She took a few steps to where Shyamita was sitting, slumped, on the bed. She gave her shoulder a squeeze and said, 'I'm right here if you need me, Shyamu. You know that, right?'

Shyamita nodded quietly.

14

Jai was pacing in the lobby of the hotel where his mother and sister were staying when his cell phone began to buzz. Looking at the caller ID his mood darkened even further. The call was from Bangalore, and he knew only too well who was calling. He promised himself that he would not tell his mother and upset her. She had been through enough and more. Besides, there really was nothing to tell her. That man had called, and he hadn't answered. And that was that.

Jai had something else that was plaguing his mind at the moment. Mithi. He flinched as he recalled the hurt look in her eyes when he had said that he would drop her off at Geet's. After the time that they had had, he had gone and foolishly screwed it up. *Self-preservation sucks, Nair*...he said to himself. But he didn't want anybody's pity. *Never wanted it then, didn't want it now!*

When he'd woken up that morning he should have realized that something had happened last night and that was why they were both sleeping on the floor. He should have known from the way Mithi was sleeping next to him that she had witnessed his nightly terrors. And for Jai, it was the most humiliating moment in his entire life when Mithi had held his face in her hands and whispered softly that everything would be all right. His pride had been badly bruised by that single line. She had said it out of the goodness of her heart, but to Jai, in that moment it had felt like pity. He didn't want her sympathy. He didn't want her to take care of him.

But then he had gone and done a mighty fine job of showing her just how much he cared about her and how much he wanted to take care of her. He hadn't even called or texted her all evening. He knew he was in the wrong here, Jai knew that very well. But…

'Aaaghhh! I shouldn't have let her go,' he cursed out loud just as the elevator doors opened and his mother and sister stepped out into the lobby.

'Shouldn't have let who go?' Naina asked, a little too eagerly.

Jai gave her what he hoped to be a dirty look before saying, 'Not in the mood, Naina.'

She gave him her own version of the dirty look before saying, 'I don't really care, Jai. You screwed up again, didn't you?'

It was times like these when Jai felt like wringing his sister's scrawny neck. Since he was pretty sure his mother would not approve of her son throttling her daughter, he simply smiled, albeit in a slightly menacing manner, and said, 'We're going to be late if we don't leave now,' saying that he began walking towards the exit doors on the far end of the lobby.

His mobile phone rang again. Jai rejected the call and switched off his phone.

Shyamita checked her phone one last time before heading down. There wasn't a single call or text from Jai. But she knew he had called and spoken to Karan in the afternoon. She had seen the latter's phone ring during lunchtime and had quickly snuck a peek at the caller-ID. Her heart had sunk further. He had called Karan, but not thought of calling her.

But Shyamita forced herself to be calm and composed. She knew Jai with his mother and sister would be coming for the evening ceremony. There was one last paath before the wedding, and the Chaddas had decided to organize it in their own house rather than dragging the entire wedding party to the gurdwara for another all-nighter. The wedding was all set to take place two nights later. Quickly checking her Patiala suit in the mirror, she gave herself a last onceover, before heading down to the main hall where about a hundred Punjabis had gathered.

'Satsriyakaal, auntyji,' she greeted Geet's mother-in-law as she entered the hall only to come to a staggering halt when she saw Jai on the other side of the room talking to Karan. In a cream kurta-pajama, with the sleeves rolled up to his elbows revealing hands that had been all over her not too long ago, Shyamita could feel herself turning red once again.

What is the matter with me? Wasn't I just crying my eyes out in the afternoon over this man and now one look at him and all I can think of is the previous night?

'Should I just kill him for you?' Geet whispered next to her and Shyamita almost had a heart attack.

'Geet! You scared me,' she said breathlessly.

'Oh, please. Just stop thinking about him, Shyamu,' Geet said softly.

What must she be thinking of me? Jai knew he had to go over to Shyamita and at least attempt to explain to her why he had behaved so deplorably. But she had a T-Rex standing right next to her. So he waited until Geet was asked to sit with Karan for the paath before he made his way to Shyamita.

Clad in a peach-coloured plain Patiala suit, with no make-up and her hair left to hang around her shoulders in loose waves, she was mesmerizing; simple, yet beautiful. And this is how Jai had always liked her. Her simplicity was her most beautiful quality.

Standing just a few feet behind her, he tapped lightly on her shoulder before saying, 'Mithi?'

Shyamita didn't respond. Instead she took a few steps further and stood next to Geet's cousin, who, if Jai was not wrong, had just landed from Canada.

'Hi,' she told him a little too breathlessly and much to Jai's annoyance.

At first, the young sardar was taken aback by Shyamita's sudden appearance next to him. But he quickly recovered from the shock and said, 'Hey, I'm Amandeep,' and extended his hand.

Jai wanted to throttle young Amandeep Chadda as he saw Shyamita shake hands with him saying, 'I'm Shyamita.'

'You're Geet's best friend. I've heard so much about you from her,' the lad was already besotted, Jai could make out from the way he was talking. 'You live in Paris, right?'

'Yes, Amandeep. I live in Paris,' Shyamita smiled at him. Jai saw red.

'Oh, that is wonderful. And please don't call me Amandeep. My friends call me Mandy.'

And Jai burst out laughing.

Shyamita would have also laughed but then she remembered she was mad at Jai, and simply smiled at Amandeep. No way was she going to call him Mandy.

She excused herself and walked over to the dining room where refreshments were being laid out. Gulping down a glass of ice-cold water, she was just about to turn around and go back to the hall when she bumped into Jai. His arm quickly shot out to steady her. She tried to pull herself free but he wouldn't let go off her arm.

'What do you want, Jai?' she bristled.

'I need to talk to you, Mithi,' he said a bit too sternly.

Shyamita's eyes narrowed at him and he could see that he would have to be a little more placating if he wanted to talk to her.

'Okay, listen, Mithi,' he started, but she stopped him saying, 'Jai, I don't want to hear anything. Can you please let go of me?'

'No,' he was stern again.

'No?' her eyes rounded.

'No,' stern again.

She hesitated for a second or two before saying, 'I have nothing to say to you. Nor do I want to listen to anything you have to say.' And with that, she stomped off towards the stairs. When she reached the top, she turned back to face him and said, 'And don't call me Mithi.'

Shyamita knew exactly who was knocking on her door. She knew Jai was standing on the other side, waiting for her to open the door and let him in. But she was scared. She was hurting. And it was Jai's fault.

'Mithi, c'mon, please open the door,' he said from the other side, his voice was slightly muffled but she could hear the desperation in it.

Shyamita stood with her back pressed against the door and tried very hard to stop her tears. 'Jai, please,' her voice cracked, 'please go away, Jai.'

'Mithi, are you crying?' he asked, worriedly. 'Just let me in, sweetheart, please.'

'Jai…I…I really…,' the tears began to fall uncontrollably now.

'Mithi, open the door, please,' Jai continued to plead.

Shyamita wiped her tears and turned to open the door. She slid the bolt free and the door sprang open. Jai stood on the opposite side, anxious and worried. Stepping into the room, he closed the door behind him and reached out to her.

'Mithi…,' he hesitated and took a couple of steps towards her. He saw her big chocolate brown eyes swimming in tears and cursed himself to Hades. He'd hurt her. He knew he should have come sooner to try and make amends. But he just couldn't figure out what he should tell her. *Where would I even begin?*

He cupped her face in his hands and pulled her closer to him. There, standing at the doorstep of her bedroom, he kissed her lightly on the forehead and pulled her into his embrace. Shyamita went willingly. She was still mad at him. She was still hurting. But she needed him.

She loved him.

They made love again. Anger, fear, pain and hurt…all was forgotten in those few moments of passionate disregard and abandon. Here, in their own world, there was nothing to hinder them. Nothing unwanted or untoward lurking in the shadows. No secrets.

It was the buzzing of Shyamita's cell phone that brought them back to reality.

'Oh, no,' was Shyamita's immediate reaction as she jumped out of the bed and ran to the dresser to answer the call. It was Michael. She turned her back to Jai and spoke.

'Hey Michael,' she said, trying to control her breathing. 'That's wonderful. Congratulations to you and Mia. I can't wait to see my godson...yes, I'll see you soon. Take care. *Au revoir*.'

She placed her cell phone back on the dresser and turned around to face Jai. He was still in bed, head propped up on his hand. He was watching Shyamita carefully. A flurry of emotions ran across her face. He knew that she was very happy for her friend, but somewhere, deep down, he could sense a melancholy in her. In an effort to distract her, in a teasing voice he said, 'Mithi, if you stand like that any longer, I'm afraid we'll have to go in for round two. And I don't think we have that kind of time.'

The result was just as he had expected. Suddenly realizing that she was still naked, Shyamita turned scarlet and then practically ran to the bed. She pulled the duvet and wrapped it around herself. For his part, Jai was quite happy the way he was, unashamedly naked.

'Jai, this was a mistake. It should never have happened.' Shyamita's voice was firm, but he could sense the insincerity of her words.

'Mithi,' he said and pulled her on to the bed, duvet and all. She landed right on top of him. 'Mithi, I don't believe that you believe this was a mistake. This was anything but a mistake. By calling it a mistake, you are making a mistake. And I don't think you're the kind of girl who makes mistakes,' he ended, smiling at her.

'This is not funny, Jairam Nair,' this time Shyamita's tone brooked no argument and she tried to get off him. But Jai wrapped his arms around her and held her tighter. 'Jai, stop,' she squirmed.

'Mithi, if you keep squirming and struggling against me, there's going to be an explosion of sorts,' he added for good measure. And that got Shyamita to lie still on top of him.

'Tell me what is bothering you,' he said.

'Nothing is bothering me, Jai,' she returned, half-heartedly.

'Mithi, I don't think there's anybody other than perhaps your parents who know you as well as I do. And since they are not here at the moment, I believe I'm the authority now,' he continued, trying to coax her to open up.

'Jai, it's nothing. Please, let it go,' she would not budge.

'Mithi, I…,' he started but she surprised by cutting him short and jumping out of his hold.

'No, Jai. Just stop, please. I need to go downstairs.' She gathered her scattered clothes and walked into the bathroom.

She emerged ten minutes later, checked her appearance in the mirror and said to him, 'Please switch off the lights on your way out,' and walked out of the room.

15

A mistake? It was a colossal mistake! How could I have done this?

Shyamita was ashamed. As she entered the hall where the paath was still going on, a few people smiled at her and a few others whispered. Did they know what she had just done? Could they guess?

With as much dignity as she could muster, she held her head high and walked towards where Geet and Karan were conversing. They had finished their part in tonight's rituals and were indulging in idle chit-chat. But as Shyamita closed in on them she caught bits of their conversation.

'She has a right to know, Karan,' came Geet's voice.

'Jai will tell her when he has to. You don't butt in,' Karan countered.

'Don't talk to me like that idiot,' Geet retaliated.

Karan sighed. 'Geet, there are more important things happening here.'

'No. Nothing is more important than Shyamita's happiness. She's been through enough,' Geet was all about championing her friend's cause.

'Don't you think Jai has been through enough? He deserves a shot at happiness,' Karan was obviously championing *his* friend's cause.

'Fine,' Geet finally gave in. 'But tell him not to hurt Shyamu. I will rip him to shreds if he does,' she said dramatically.

'I think he knows exactly what you're capable of, you little imp,' Karan laughed and pulled her into his arms.

'By the way,' Geet whispered, 'I love the Archies' card you sent me this morning.'

'Are you blushing, Geet?' Karan teased her. 'I'm glad the words in the card had their desired effect. Do you think we can try one of those things during the honeymoon?' he asked his fiancée.

'We can try all that and much more,' she whispered while giggling and Karan kissed the top of her head, laughing softly.

Not wanting to spoil their moment and already having heard enough of their conversation for her brain cells to work overtime, Shyamita slinked back into a corner and stood there alone, processing all that she had just heard.

What was going on here? Clearly there was something Jai had not told her, but that Geet and Karan were aware of. She could just ask Geet and she was sure her friend would tell her whatever it was. But then she also agreed with what Karan had said. Jai would tell her when he had to. *But what was the big secret anyway?*

She ran her eyes over the gathering and spotted his mother and sister. They were seated right behind 'Mandy' from Canada. Naina was talking animatedly to her mother. Shyamita noticed that Lalita Aunty was not really listening to whatever her daughter was saying. Every now and then she'd smile as if to say that she was paying attention to Naina's ramblings. But then, in the very next second, a sort of melancholy would settle on her expression.

Shyamita felt utterly helpless. She wanted to go over to Lalita Aunty and comfort her that whatever was bothering her would go away soon. But she knew nothing of her troubles. In school, Jai had always been an introvert and very rarely shared anything personal about himself or his family. Shyamita along with Geet had been the loud ones. Which was perhaps why Jai knew everything about her and her family, whilst she knew so little about him. He would never even talk to her about his family. She knew that his mother and father were estranged. But the reason for the estrangement was not known to her. And she had not probed further when he had accidentally let it slip during lunch one afternoon in the school cafeteria.

Now as she stood watching his mother she realized that there was a lot more going on that she was not aware of. *And perhaps would never be aware of,* a small voice hissed in her head.

Jai walked in then, scanning the room for Shyamita. He spotted her sitting by the windowsill and staring out into the night. He walked over to his mother and sister, asking them if they wanted anything before walking over to Shyamita.

Shyamita sensed Jai's nearness and turned to face him. Before he could say anything she said, 'I am sorry, Jai. I shouldn't have walked out like that,' her voice shook as she said it.

He smiled, offered her his arm and asked, 'Walk with me?'

The night sky was black. The stars and moon had decided not to make an appearance, almost as if they too could sense the melancholy. There was a light breeze blowing, but the air was damp and heavy. *Mumbai's famous humidity*, Shyamita thought.

Jai was silent and Shyamita was at a loss for words. She had apologized to him for her dismal behavior, but she had not been able to say anything more than that. They stopped when they reached the garden bench. The area was fairly well lit. Shyamita was still holding onto his arm as they sat down on the bench, an unspoken distance between the two. For the longest time, neither of them said anything. It was as if the distance had eaten up whatever words they had to say.

Sooner or later this was going to happen, the niggling voice shouted inside Shyamita's head and she shook her head vehemently.

'What is it?' Jai asked her.

'Nothing,' came her reply.

Silence again. Shyamita could hear the vehicles moving in the busy streets outside Geet's house. That was another aspect that was typical to Mumbai. No matter the hour, the streets would always be bustling with noisy vehicles. Paris wasn't like this. The city did eventually go to sleep.

'Mithi, do you really believe what happened some time ago was a mistake?' Jai's questions shattered through her thoughts. She could hear the hurt in his voice. Clearly that one word she had used had got to him. She had to correct it.

'Jai, I only said that out of anger,' she started to explain, but he cut in, 'And so you called it a mistake?'

'No, Jai, I...'

'Mithi, it was not a mistake for me,' he didn't give her a chance to complete. 'I don't know what has got into you, but you cannot write us off as a mistake.'

This time, Shyamita cut him short. Barely managing to restrain her temper, she shucked off his arm and said, 'what has got into me? Are you seriously asking me that? After the way you behaved this morning, you seriously expect me to answer that, Jairam Nair?'

'I'm sorry for this morning,' he said in a small, barely audible whisper.

'You're sorry? Are you really? Is that why you came looking for a tumble in the sack this evening?' Shyamita's voice was almost matching Geet's supersonic decibels.

They were lucky they were far from the house, deep in the gardens.

'Will you even give me a chance to talk?' he asked her, exasperated now.

'No. I honestly don't want to hear anything you have to say. You have said and done more than enough.' She got up from the bench and took a few steps away before turning back and saying, 'No, strike that. You don't say anything. You never talk to me about anything. You're a closed book, Jai,' she laughed then, 'How ironic is that? A bestselling author who is too afraid to speak his mind. Wow!'

Jai was stunned into silence, but apparently Shyamita was not done. She took a deep, calming breath and walked back to the bench. She sat down again, and in a much softer voice said, 'Jai, we've been friends for more than half our lives. But there is so much that I don't know about you, your family. You've never shared anything with me. Whereas you know everything about me. I cannot go on like this. I need more. You have to let me in. You have to let people in. Are you afraid that whatever happened to your parents will happen to us?'

That was enough for Jai. He'd heard enough. He didn't want to hear anymore. Shyamita had just laid out his biggest fear so easily and openly in front of him. And she didn't know the worst part of it. He couldn't do this to her anymore, she was right. He had to let her go. This time, for her own good. He wouldn't let her drown in the same abyss. He just had to let her go.

He cupped her face in his hands, wanting to feel her softness one last time. His heart was shattering into a million pieces. But he knew he could not give her what she wanted. His fear had taken him over completely. He kissed her on her mouth and crushed her to his chest. Breathing in the scent of her hair, *her* scent...his Mithi, for one last time.

'I am sorry, Mithi,' he whispered softly and kissed her on her forehead, one last time.

He pulled back, got up from the bench and walked away. Retrieving his mobile phone from his kurta's pocket, he texted Karan and told him to take his mother and sister to their hotel when the paath was over. Then, he got into his car and drove away.

In the side-view mirror he could see Shyamita's reflection becoming smaller and finally disappearing as he turned onto the main road. He had let her go.

16

Half an hour later, Geet found Shyamita sitting on the garden-bench. Something was wrong. She could sense it.

'Shyamu?' she ventured as she sat down next to her friend. 'Shyamu, is everything okay? Where is Jai?'

Shyamita did not respond. She just sat there, mum.

'Shyamu, baby, tell me what's wrong? Why are you sitting here alone?' Geet was getting worried now.

No response.

'Do you want to go inside?' she asked.

Nothing.

'Did Jai say something to you?' Geet was trying her level best to remain calm when she noticed tears pooling in Shyamita's eyes. 'I knew it!' she burst out. 'That moron did something, didn't he? What'd he do? Did he hurt you? I'm going to kill him. Where is he?'

Just as Geet stood up to go in search of 'the moron', in a soft, barely audible whisper, Shyamita said, 'He's gone, Geet.'

'Where has he gone?' she asked Shyamita.

'He's just...*gone*.' And she burst into tears.

If Geet could have consoled Shyamita and strangled Jai at the same time, she would have been one hugely satisfied woman. But alas, she could not do both. So for now, she comforted her friend. She held Shyamita as she sobbed her heart out. She whispered sweet but empty words of reassurance to her that everything would be alright, knowing full well that nothing would change unless a certain pig-headed Malayali changed. She helped Shyamita to her feet and took her back into the house through the kitchen door. She then helped her up the stairs to her room. All that while, Shyamita was sobbing silently. Finally, Geet tucked her into bed, kissed her on her forehead, turned off the lights and shut the door to her bedroom.

She then went in search of her fiancé.

Jai felt absolutely horrible. He hated himself. He hated himself for having hurt Shyamita. He shouldn't have ended things the way he had. He could have handled it better.

Not for the first time in four days, Jai wished he was not a teetotaller. He needed to drown himself. He wanted to forget about the misery he had caused Shyamita. But he knew no amount of alcohol would give him the oblivion he craved. On his way home, he'd cursed himself and the wicked hand that fate had dealt him. Shyamita was right. He never shared. He couldn't stand pity. And he would never be able to bear it if Shyamita were to pity him. He didn't want it. But he also didn't want to hurt her. And that is exactly what he had done. He had hurt her. Again.

What else am I supposed to do? She would continue to get hurt by him and that was something he did not want to have on his conscience. So, this was the best solution. *Right?*

Are you afraid that whatever happened to your parents will happen to us? Those were her words; spoken so innocently but she had no idea how close to home her remark had been. Yes, that was his biggest fear. He'd never witnessed a happy family life. Some people were just lucky, he wasn't one of them.

His mother had been through so much in her life. And she had had no choice but to bear it all because she had two young children to take care of and a family who said they would refuse to acknowledge her existence if she left her husband. So she had borne it all, until one fine day, her son had pulled her out of it.

His mobile phone began to buzz again. It was his mother, probably calling to say that she and Naina were back in their hotel.

'Hi, Amma,' his voice was hoarse.

'Jai...,' his mother sobbed into the phone. And he knew. He knew why there had been so many calls from Bangalore all day.

His father was dead.

Shyamita opened her eyes to find Geet sleeping soundly next to her. She smiled in spite of herself. Trust Geet to be her guardian angel even while she was asleep. In school, Geet had always been the one to cover up for her, help her with all the assignments she would miss because of her dance concerts and sometimes even do her homework for her. She had missed Geet all these years. She had always been more like a sister to her. And Shyamita realized she needed her friend, now more than ever.

Her heart had been broken twice. And both times by the same man – Jai. She wanted to be mad at him; she wanted to hate him. But she couldn't bring herself to do that.

No matter what, you'll always be the one I love, Jairam Nair.

But now, those words, those feelings they did not even matter. Because she had ceased to matter for him. He had taken the easy way out, hadn't he? He had decided what was best, according to him, for both of them. Jai would never let her in. She would never know what *he* wanted.

Did you ever love me, Jai? Her broken heart cried.

She closed her eyes and remembered their train meeting twelve years ago, the first time she had had her heart broken.

She had asked Jai if Aisha was his girlfriend. For a long while he didn't say anything. And then finally, he had said, 'If that is what you think, Mithi, then I have nothing to say to you. You obviously know me quite well, it would seem.' He placed the two cups of ice cream on her seat, turned on his heel and walked out of the compartment and out of her life.

Beside her, Geet stirred. 'Shyamu?' she croaked.

'Hmm?'

'Are you okay?' she asked Shyamita, worry and concern evident in her voice.

'I'm fine, Geet,' Shyamita replied, trying to sound nonchalant, but failing miserably as her voice shook.

'If it's any consolation, I'm going to kill Jai when I see him tonight,' Geet assured her.

Shyamita bolted out of bed. 'Jai's going to be here tonight?' she almost screeched.

'Umm...yes, he's Karan's friend too. So I can't kick him out,' Geet replied sheepishly.

Shyamita didn't know what to say.

'Are you going to be okay seeing him, Shyamu?' she sat up in bed, crossed her legs and eyed her friend keenly.

'No...I...mean err...yeah, I should be fine,' Shyamita's voice shook.

'I could make Karan tell him not to come,' she offered.

'No,' Shyamita replied quickly, 'I don't want you and Karan to have problems because of this, Geet. You've done enough for me, really,' her eyes were brimming with tears now.

'Shyamu, you come first for me. You know that, right?' Geet was on the verge of tears herself.

In one quick motion, Shyamita leapt onto the bed and hugged her friend. Together, the two girls cried, laughed and then cried some more.

But all too soon, Geet was called downstairs to get ready for a visit to her in-laws's place. Shyamita told her that she wouldn't be joining the family for lunch.

'Where are you going, Shyamu?' Geet asked.

'I'm going to school,' came Shyamita's response.

'Sunil kaka, how are you?' Shyamita asked the old man who sitting on a bench outside the principal's office, her Marathi slightly rusty. The old man peered at her through his large black rectangular glasses, which were rather too big for his small bald head. 'Who are you?' he asked, his voice all wheezy.

'Arre, Sunil kaka, how could you forget me?' Shyamita continued in Marathi. The old man continued to stare at her. Finally, he stood up, shaking his head. Bent because of his age, his back was almost parallel to the floor. But he was the school's most beloved member of staff which was perhaps why he was still there despite his old age, arthritis, and a multitude of other ailments.

After finding a proper foothold, he looked up at Shyamita and caught hold of her hand. Giving it a gentle squeeze, he said, 'You are Jai's Shyamita, aren't you?'

Tears clogged at the back of Shyamita's throat. So apparently the whole world knew and remembered her as 'Jai's Shyamita'. But the man in question refused to think of her in that light.

Stopping herself from wallowing in self-pity, she smiled at kaka and said, 'Yes, kaka. I am Shyamita.' The old man gave her his most charming toothless grin. 'How are you,

Mithu?' He called her by the name he had given her. 'Still as naughty as ever?' he grinned.

After meeting with Principal D'Mello, Shyamita walked around the school and visited some of her favorite places. The librarian, Ms Coelho, was engrossed in an Agatha Christie novel as always; Mr Cherrian, the lab-assistant was busy cleaning vials and flasks; and Ms Jacinta was teaching her class of ninth-graders. She was teaching them Shyamita's favorite novel, Jane Austen's *Pride and Prejudice.* Jai used to tease her mercilessly about the way she used to fantasize about Mr Darcy and how for the longest time she had wanted nothing more than to be 'mistress of Pemberley'.

On the far end of the school, right where the primary school section was located, there was a huge banyan tree. It was probably as old as the school. During the monsoons, she and Jai would sit under the shade of this very tree and gossip about their classmates. *Those really were the days,* Shyamita thought as she leaned against the trunk of the banyan tree and slid onto the ground. There were just a few students out on the grounds, probably punished by their respective teachers for some reason. There was still half an hour to go before the lunch bell would ring.

She thought of all the times she and Jai would bunk classes and come and sit here, under this very tree. More often than not, the PT instructor, Ram Sir would catch the two of them and would try to drag them to Principal D'Mello's office. But then, Sunil kaka would always come to their rescue. It was under this very tree that she had told Jai that she wanted to paint, but had never got the chance to pursue this passion because her parents had forced her to choose dance. She could still recall what he had said.

'So what, Mithi? Why do you have to listen to your parents?' he asked defiantly.

'Because they are my parents, Jai,' she had replied innocently.

That was perhaps the first time she had seen Jai's rebellious side. 'No, Mithi. That's really no reason to listen to them.'

'But Jai…,' she began.

'Mithi,' he said, cutting her short, 'You listen to someone who offers you good advice, not just because they're your parents or your friends or your relatives.' And then he looked at her with a strange quizzical expression on his face, 'Don't you have a mind of your own, Shyamita Bose?'

Shyamita scrunched up her nose and stuck her tongue out at him. Jai burst out laughing.

Now as Shyamita sat at the same spot she and Jai used to occupy almost every day, she smiled at her own naivety. Back then, she had thought that she was smart enough to handle anything that would come her way. She was confident in her own skin. But somehow, she had also known that her self-confidence was just a manifestation of the security she felt when she was around Jai.

'You were the one, Jairam Nair,' she said softly. She didn't allow the melancholy to settle or the tears to flow. She quickly stood up and walked over to the girls' hostel wing. There was a new matron in place of old Mrs Dias, who had succumbed to cancer a couple of years ago. The new matron, Mrs Anandan, was just as warm and welcoming as Mrs Dias had been. She offered Shyamita some snacks and tea. The plates and glasses were the same as they had been twelve years ago. Just looking at them brought back a flood of memories of the times when Geet would join her for lunch in the lunch-hall, or the time when Jai had accidentally spilled hot tea on his pants and hopped up and down like a kangaroo. The scarred tables still held the names of students. On the far end of the big mahogany table, four names had been inscribed with the help of a compass – Jai, Shyamita, Geet and Karan. So much had changed since then, and yet, things were still the same. Geet and Karan, still together, now they were getting married. Jai and Shyamita were still unable to express their feelings and so together, had managed to screw things up for good.

Shyamita didn't have time to ponder over this for too long. The lunch-bell rang and soon there would be students rushing into the lunch-hall. This was her chance to go and meet her favorite teacher. She'd be sitting in the staffroom with the biology teacher, exchanging notes on which student did what today. How she'd yearned for Ms Jacinta's advice during all the times she'd struggled hard to hold herself together.

Shyamita knocked on the staffroom door and some of the teachers looked up. But only one yelled, 'Shyamita Bose, is that really you?'

17

Ten years ago, when Jai had come home from Cardiff during his summer break, things had not been looking good in the Nair household. But soon enough they got worse and he walked out leaving behind his mother and younger sister, who was also home for the holidays. Since then, not a day had gone by when he hadn't thought of home. The two months of his summer break he stayed at a paying guest accommodation just outside of Domlur district in Bangalore. Every night, he would cry himself to sleep. His mother would plead with him to come home, but he would refuse. He knew he was being difficult. He knew his mother and sister needed him. But he couldn't stand the thought of being in the same house with his father anymore. He had borne enough. He wanted out. But at the same time, he also knew that he had to support his mother in every possible way. There were nights when he would wake up screaming and it would take all seven of his flatmates to calm him down. He would dream of the agony he'd been through during his childhood, before his grandfather had died and left his mother enough money to send him to boarding school in Mumbai. Naina was sent to live with Jai's spinster aunt in Kochi.

When Jai was younger, not a day went by when his father didn't strike him, whip him, or burn him. Drunk and unemployed, his father would take out all his frustration on his wife and son. Jai's mother was a school teacher and it was on her salary that the family survived. When Jai was much younger he had vowed to himself that he would support his mother in every way he could. He knew she had sent him away to boarding school so that he wouldn't have to bear the atrocities that his father would undoubtedly inflict on him.

Three days before his nineteenth birthday, Jai had walked in to see his father trying to force himself on his mother. Disgusted and repelled, he yanked the man off his screaming mother. When his father moved to strike him, Jai caught him by his neck. The old man nearly choked before Jai's mother pushed him away and he let go of his father's neck.

'See the bastard you have spawned,' his father spat at his mother.

Tears in her eyes, his mother had begged him, 'Jai, apologize to Appa.'

Stunned that his mother still couldn't stand up for herself, he said, 'No. I will not.'

'Just look at the venom in his eyes,' his father barked, 'He would have killed me.'

'Yes,' Jai said, straight-faced. 'You touch Amma again, and I will kill you.'

Jai saw his father's face turn from red to purple. But he didn't care.

'Don't look at me like that. You touch Amma or Naina ever again and I will kill you.'

Those were the last words he spoke to his father. Over the years, he had called his mother and asked her to leave his father many times. But not once did she listen. His house in Mumbai was for his mother. But she refused to stay with him. Whenever she visited him, she would stay in a hotel. He knew she did it out of respect for her husband. But the man did not deserve even a smidgen of the respect his wife continued to give him. Naina would stay with her brother, but their mother never did. The Indian society and family mentality was such. His mother would not be seen as the victim. Rather, they would accuse her of being selfish. He also knew that at one time, his mother had truly loved his father. Perhaps, that was the reason why she had never been able to leave him. After he had published his first bestseller, he had bought a small apartment for his mother in the Bannerghata area of Bangalore, but she had refused to move.

'This is my home, Jai. It will always be my home,' she had told him when he had called to give her the news.

And today, ten years later, he was back in the same house. Emotions he had suppressed for nearly a decade came out when he entered his old room. The posters of the then famous cricketers and wrestlers were still adorning the walls. His cot, which he had pushed closer to the window, one very hot summer, was still there, albeit slightly worse for wear and with a dusty mattress. Across the bed stood his large steel cupboard with a gazillion photos of his mother, sister, his friends in Bangalore and Shyamita.

He sauntered to his cupboard and ran his fingers across the photographs. One particular photo stood out. It was a photo of Shyamita he had taken during the only dance performance he had ever attended. He'd hated the way some of the boys from school had been passing remarks and commenting about her. He'd wanted to strangle each of them. Instead, he decided he wouldn't ever attend any other concerts. Looking at the photo now, he realized how much Mithi had changed since then. She was no longer the bold and outgoing kind. Now she was quiet and more reserved. In school, she used to be a brat. She would even bully some of the boys. But now, she spoke only when spoken to. She'd changed so much. Was it because of her accident? Somewhere, deep down, Jai knew the answer. But he refused to acknowledge it now. The time had passed. He had let her go.

Looking at the photograph again, he asked himself, 'Have I done the right thing?'

After the last rites were performed, Jai, along with his uncle and cousin walked back home. When he walked in,

Jai found his aunts comforting and consoling his mother. But Jai couldn't bring himself to feel any kind of remorse or sadness. True, he didn't have a father anymore. But for the longest time, he had considered Amma to be both his mother and father. Soon, the house was teeming with relatives and friends pouring in to offer their condolences. Jai sat next to his sister on the couch in the hall while his mother was sitting on the divan, flanked by her sisters-in-law. Like him, his sister was also not overly distraught; she too was secretly relieved that their mother was finally able to live her life freely and without any kind of guilt.

Presently, Naina leaned over to her brother and whispered, 'Jai, will you be taking Amma back with you to Mumbai?'

'I don't know if she'll come right away,' he told her in a low tone. He didn't want the rest of the family to know what they were talking about.

'Yes, but, you'll take her anyway, right?' Naina persisted.

Jai looked at his sister quizzically, 'I don't know, Naina,' he answered, exasperated. 'I will have to see how to manage the move. It will be difficult for Amma to adjust to life in Mumbai.'

'Yes, but she'll have Shyamita to help her,' his sister supplied and that made Jai's frown deepen.

'Shyamita? What does she have to do with this?' Jai asked, now openly curious.

'Sshh…! Lower your voice, Jairam Nair,' she admonished him, as if he were the younger sibling and continued,

'You're going to ask her to marry you,' and then noticing her brother's crestfallen expression, she asked, 'aren't you?' She gasped, 'what did you do, Jai?'

'What do you mean, what have I done? I did nothing,' he said indignantly.

'Obviously you did nothing,' she said irritably and got up and stomped off in the direction of the kitchen.

Jai watched his sister's retreating figure and wondered for the second time that day – *have I done the right thing?*

There was a sharp knock on Shyamita's door. She knew it was Geet on the other side come to help her get dressed for the evening. The bride-to-be had rushed through her make-up and dress-sitting, so that she could spend as much time as she possibly could with her friend, who was nursing a broken heart. Shyamita was grateful to Geet; for if she hadn't been there, nothing would have stopped Shyamita from completely breaking down. Geet had held her while she had bawled her eyes out.

She scrambled off the bed and ran to open the door. Geet stood on the other side wearing a beautiful shimmering baby-pink sequined anarkali suit and silver high-heeled strappy sandals. She wore her hair in a long simple braid and the end of the braid was held together by decorative tassels known as parandi.

'Why aren't you dressed yet?' she cried as she barged into Shyamita's room.

'I'm not coming, Geet,' Shyamita said in a small voice.

'What do you mean you're not coming, Shyamita Bose?' Geet was going to reach supersonic decibel levels very soon.

'I don't feel like it, I'm sorry,' Shyamita added quickly.

'You don't feel like it?' Geet's voice was almost there. 'You don't FEEL like it?!?!?' *There*!

'Geet, will you just relax?' Shyamita tried to calm her down. But the other girl was impossible to placate.

'Look here, Shyamu,' she started, 'I did not come up here to argue with you. I want you to be with me tonight. Please,' she was pleading now. 'I did not say anything when you ditched the lunch at Karan's house and went to visit school instead. But I am not going to let you sit cooped up in this room all evening either. I'm sorry, Shyamu. I really am. I can only imagine what you must be going through right now,' she sighed, tears collecting in her eyes as she said, 'But can you, just this once, just for tonight, forget about Jai and celebrate with me? I'm getting married, Shyamu. Please?'

Shyamita felt horrible. Here she was, moping and sulking about somebody who hadn't even bothered to call or text her all day, instead of being happy for her closest and dearest friend. *How can you be so selfish, Shyamita!* She cursed herself.

'I'm sorry, Geet,' she said softly, and crossed over to where Geet was now sitting on the bed and scrubbing away the tears that were now freely flowing down her cheeks. 'I'm such an idiot. I've just been so selfish. I haven't thought about you. I'm really sorry,' she laid her head on Geet's shoulder. Within seconds, Geet brought her head to rest on top of Shyamita's.

They sat like that for a while. Just happy in each other's company; in each other's solitude. Then Shyamita said in a teasing voice, 'I hope you're wearing waterproof mascara.' And Geet laughed.

Not coming tonight, bro. Something's come up. Amma and Naina are with me. Will explain when I get back. Take care. J.

Karan stabbed the standby button on his phone and got into his car. He had not seen Jai all day, hadn't even heard from him all day. Then when Karan finally called Jai to ask him where he was and if he was alright, the arrogant moron, instead of answering his cell phone, sends him this text. Revving the engine of his 7 series BMW, Karan got into the heavy Mumbai traffic that he would have to wade through in order to get to Geet's house. His fiancée had called him in the morning and told him that she was going to wring his friend's neck when she saw him in the evening. But unfortunately for Geet (and fortunately for Jai), that was not going to happen. Karan had half a mind to call up Naina and ask her what the hell was going on. But he knew

Jai wouldn't like it. The man was weird like that. He was arrogant and weird.

Karan had seen how distraught Shyamita had been the night before. And he'd also found out what had transpired between Jai and Shyamita. Honestly, at that time, all he wanted to do was to join Geet in finding Jai and throwing him off the Sea Link. When he'd gone back to the hotel last night, he'd hoped to find Jai waiting for them in the lobby. But Jai was nowhere to be seen. He tried calling him on his mobile phone, but he couldn't get through. This morning too, he had been unable to reach Jai. All afternoon he'd been frantic with worry. He had been seriously considering calling Naina when he received Jai's text message. What the hell was he going to explain when he got back?

He had to tell Shyamita. The poor girl was going to be heartbroken again.

18

So Jai was not going to attend tonight's party. *That's a good thing.* The voice in Shyamita's head was trying to convince her that this was what she had wanted too. Karan had been fumbling with his words when he had told her that he'd received a text from Jai saying he would not be coming. And Shyamita's heart had shattered further, if that was even possible.

'Err...Shyamu, I uh...here's the thing...umm...,' Karan had fumbled without making eye contact.

'What is it, Karan?' she'd asked him softly.

'Shyamu...err...Jai...,' he began, but Shyamita cut him short. 'Is he coming?'

'Umm...no, Shyamu. He sent me a text saying he isn't.' No sooner were the words out of Karan's mouth, than he saw Shyamita's face fall. The fake smile she had plastered on her face for his benefit faltered. 'Shyamu, listen to me,' he said, 'Jai is a moron. Don't let him pull you down, okay?'

Shyamita said nothing, but just nodded. 'Good girl,' Karan smiled at her and led her to where Geet was standing, talking to her brood of cousins. He wanted nothing more in this world than to have Jai walk in through the front door just so that he could smash his face. He knew Shyamita was putting on a brave front for Geet's sake, but he could see the anguish and pain the poor girl was in. He knew that she loved Jai to bits. He also knew that the idiot loved her equally, if not more. But right now, he felt absolutely helpless and useless.

They were really done this time, weren't they?

Shyamita plastered a smile on her face for Geet's sake and stepped onto the garden lawn where the Chaddas and Walias had assembled for the dance party. Tonight was the last function at Geet's house that was being attended by both the families. Tomorrow afternoon and evening, there were events planned at Karan's parents' house. While the mehndi ceremony would begin tomorrow morning at Geet's house.

Shyamita walked over to where Geet was standing with her mother and cousins. Neetu Aunty launched into conversation immediately, 'you look very beautiful, Shyamu. This color suits you.' Shyamita was wearing a sea-green, knee-length, sleeveless cocktail dress, with a scooped neckline. Her feet were encased in gold strappy sandals and the only jewellery she wore was a pair of gold hoop earrings. 'Thank you, Neetu Aunty,' she smiled and added, 'you look as radiant as ever.'

The older woman blushed, kissed Shyamita on her forehead, and then walked across to Karan's parents, leaving Shyamita and Geet alone for the moment.

'Did that moron text you?' Geet was on the attack immediately.

'No. And I don't want to talk about him,' Shyamita countered.

'If I was in your place, Shyamu, I'd have broken his nose,' her friend was relentless.

'But you're not. So let's leave his nose as it is,' Shyamita replied, desperately trying to maintain her composure.

'Oh, alright,' Geet finally gave in, 'Let's enjoy tonight.'

Right, enjoy!

She would at least *try* to enjoy. For Geet's sake.

'Oh, my god! You said that?' Naina was furious at her brother.

'Don't look at me like that,' Jai said quickly, 'Of course I had to say that.'

'But, Jai, she loves you,' she said before adding, 'how can you not see that?'

'She does not love me, Naina,' he said with such incredulous certainty that Naina burst out laughing.

They were sitting in the kitchen and eating raw mangoes like they used to when they were children. Amma was finally sleeping after all the guests and relatives had left.

'There's nothing to laugh about,' Jai's voice rode with his anger.

'Shh! You'll wake Amma,' his sister admonished. She popped a small piece of mango into her mouth before saying, 'Look, Jai. You have to get over whatever happened between Amma and Appa. You are not him. Why can't you see that?'

'I don't want to talk about this, Naina,' he said and pushed his plate aside. He got up to leave but his sister caught his hand and said, 'No, you have to.'

'Naina!' he warned.

'Shut up, Jai. I'm not going to stop talking just because you glower and yell at me,' she said adamantly. 'You have to get one thing straight into that thick and fat skull of yours. You. Are. Not. Appa. And you can never be him. You are too kind and generous and good to be like him,' she smiled.

Naina knew her brother's insecurities lay way deeper than that. She knew that his emotional scarring stemmed from his belief that he had not been able to do anything for their mother. She also understood that it would be a huge step for Jai to let someone into his world, which had always comprised of just the three of them. For a while, when he had been in school, their mother had believed that Shyamita would be able to pull him out of the abyss that he had doomed himself to. But then, young and immature as they were, they threw away whatever feelings they had for each other. At least her brother did, Naina knew. She knew that Shyamita still loved Jai. But she had to make her stubborn brother realize that he loved her too. And she had to do this before Shyamita went back to Paris.

The party had finally ended. There were some people who were half-crawling, half-walking back to their cars, whilst others slumped in various corners in the hall and dining room. A few of Geet's cousins who couldn't manage to climb the stairs to go to their respective rooms upstairs were sprawled on the stairs. Since Shyamita had just had a single shot of Absolut, she was still in control of her limbs. So she helped Geet upstairs to her room. The bride had gone all out today. Knowing that she wouldn't be allowed to meet Karan tomorrow, Geet had consumed nearly half a bottle of Absolut before she moved on to tequila.

After tucking her into bed, Shyamita closed her bedroom door and went into her room. She quickly undressed herself, removed the minimal make-up she had applied and washed her face. She then padded across to the dresser to check if there were any calls or texts from Jai. Nothing. There was just a text from her mother asking her if she wanted her brother, Shaunak, to pick her up from Pune station two days later and if she wanted to have fish curry and rice for lunch. She smiled at her mother's questions and quickly texted back *'Of course, Ma. What a question. I want lots of fish. And ask Shaunak to pick me up, please. See you soon. Love to you and Baba.'*

She brushed the tangles out of her hair and rummaged in her backpack for a hair-tie. Unable to find one, she picked up her backpack, walked over to the bed and started dumping its contents onto the bed. Out fell her sketchpad, her pencil-case, several sealed erasers, three hair-ties, one hair-clip and a book. It was the same one she had wanted to read at Jai's the other night - *Letters and Poems to Mother, by J. L. Nair.*

She wondered how it had managed to find its way into her backpack. Perhaps, she had mistakenly packed it along with her other things that morning when they had left home in an unspoken hurry. Not wanting to dwell on that wretched day for too long, Shyamita picked up a yellow scrunchie and gathered her curls into a high ponytail. She put her things back into her backpack, leaving Jai's book on the bed. Dumping the bag on the floor, she switched on the reading lamp that sat on the bedside table and switched off the rest of the lights. She picked up Jai's book and sank into the bed.

'Shyamita, you shouldn't be reading this,' she told herself. 'Why do you want to torture yourself thinking about him and reading what he has written?'

But a few seconds later, she said to herself, 'It'll be okay. It'll be like he's finally talking to me,' saying that she opened the book and began to read.

After half an hour of reading, Shyamita put the book down. She had read six letters and each one had been heart-wrenching. But it was the last one which had broken her heart and made her weep for the scared nine-year-old boy who had written to this mother.

This was what it said –

Mother, I am sitting underneath the kitchen sink and writing this to you. I don't know when you're going to come looking for me, but when you do please don't lie to me by saying you fell down the stairs. I know what happens to you. I have seen him hit you. I have heard your screams of pain and anguish. I cannot sleep at night because I fear if I close my eyes this is all I'm going to dream about. I want to help you, mother. I really do. But I don't know what to do. Sometimes I think of taking a knife and plunging it into that man's heart. But I know what you will say. You will say that I should not have killed my father!

But how can he be my father? He doesn't even look at me. He doesn't even care if I exist or don't. He beats me when you are not at home. But I lie to you and say that I fell while playing football with Siddharth and Arvind.

You are pregnant and he doesn't even care about the child inside you. He is not my father. He cannot be. From this day, you are my mother and father. And I promise you that the moment I am capable enough I will pull you out of this misery and give you a better life.

You will come with me, won't you?

Shyamita had always known that Jai had had a bad and disturbed childhood. But *this*...this she did not know. Her heart wept for the scared little boy. How terrified he must have been. How helpless he must have felt. She wanted to go back in time and help save the little boy, his mother and his unborn sister. She wanted to hold him tight and tell him that the world was not all bad and that he had only good inside him.

She couldn't read anymore that night. She closed the book and was about to place it on the nightstand when she noticed the initials Jai had used. She knew his father's name was Jagdish Nair. Jai's school certificates had his name as Jairam Jagdish Nair. But now, he had changed it.

Now, he was Jairam Lalita Nair. He had taken his mother's name.

Wiping her tears away, Shyamita placed the book on the nightstand, switched off the reading lamp, hugged the extra pillow tight to herself and whispered the words, 'Goodnight, Jairam Lalita Nair,' into the night.

That night, Shyamita dreamed of a little young boy crouching underneath the kitchen sink, tears pouring silently out of his eyes as he heard his mother's anguished screams coming from the next room. She woke up in a cold sweat in the early hours of the morning. Shaking from head to toe, she got out of bed and padded to the dresser and picked up the bottle of water. She quickly gulped down the water and tried to settle her nerves. But she couldn't go back to sleep. So she grabbed a shawl from her suitcase, wrapped it around herself and walked out of her bedroom.

She went down to the kitchen to find Raman kaka already up and about. The old man was humming along with the radio that was faintly playing old Hindi film songs. Shyamita recognized some of the songs. She and Jai would sing them during their visits to the seaside. She was still angry with Jai, but at least she now understood his reservations.

But he could have called you, a little voice in her head chimed not too chirpily.

Maybe he doesn't think you need to know, maybe you don't matter as much as you think, the voice said again.

'Namaste, bibi,' soft, raspy voice of Raman kaka broke Shyamita's reverie.

She smiled at the toothless old man and said, 'Good morning, kaka.' Then after a slight pause she asked him in Marathi, 'Can I help you with anything?'

Raman kaka shook his head and said, 'No, no, Shyamu bibi. You sit. I will make you some chai,' and saying that he gestured toward the short kitchen stool near the window.

Shyamita smiled at him and walked towards the window. The sun was just rising from behind the clouds. In the distance, she could see the pale white moon setting and slowly a mild orange began to seep into the darkness of the sky. It was morning. A new day.

What of it? The voice in her head was back. But Shyamita had to agree. Nothing good was going to come of the day anyway. Today, she would be home with Geet and her cousins. It was supposed to be a day just for girls, according to Geet.

Shyamita really wasn't in the mood for any kind of frivolity. But for Geet's sake she knew she had to put on her brightest smile and be there for her friend. So for now, all thoughts about Jai and whatever she had read in his book last night would have to take a backseat. She was still angry with him. She just didn't know if she had already forgiven him. *Had she?*

19

'He's not in town?' Geet bellowed into her mobile phone. She was getting her mehndi done, and so Shyamita was holding the phone to her ear. And as soon as Shyamita heard Geet's words, her heart sank.

'And why is he not in town?' Geet persisted. 'Karan Walia, you tell me what the hell is going right now. Or I'm going to come over to your place and sit on you!'

Shyamita could hear Karan's faint voice saying he did not know why Jai had left. All he knew was that Jai was currently in Bangalore.

'Fine. Whatever,' Geet said, her voice shaking in anger. 'If he so much as sets foot into the marriage hall the day after tomorrow, I will kill him with my bare hands.' Saying that, she moved her head away and Shyamita put her mobile phone on the table next to the divan on which the two of them were seated.

So Jai had left town. Well, he needn't have gone to so much trouble, she thought to herself. It's not that she was going to go over to his place and drag him out. If he did not want to speak to her and maintain any kind of contact with her, then so be it. He hadn't told her anything. As far as Jai was concerned, she was still in the dark about his family life. And she was not going to tell him anything either. Something like this, Shyamita conceded, couldn't be coerced out of a person. They had to open up on their own. Perhaps, Jai had never felt close enough to her to open up to her in the first place.

That last thought dragged Shyamita's mood down even further. Beside her, Geet was cursing Jai. 'Just let him get here. What does he think of himself? Some big-shot writer he may be. But right now, he's just an ass. Moron. Jerk.'

Shyamita couldn't take it anymore. She got up from the divan and walked over to the table that was aligned along the side wall of the hall. She poured herself a glass of ice-cold water and drank it down in one quick glug. Yes, she was miffed at Jai but that didn't mean she would take kindly to Geet's constant bashing of him. She needed some air.

But before she could excuse herself, Najma, one of the mehndi artists who had finished with Geet's cousin called out to her, 'It's your turn now, madam.' Shyamita wanted to refuse, but she feared that would sour Geet's mood further. So she gave in.

She sat down on the armchair which had been vacated by Geet's cousin and stretched out her left arm. Najma, who was barely nineteen or twenty, began drawing an intricate pattern in the middle of her palm. Shyamita's eyes followed the quick movements of Najma's hand, fascinated. After about ten minutes, the girl paused and asked Shyamita, 'whose name do you want to write?'

This was an old Indian custom, where the girl is supposed to write her beloved's name or his initials in her henna design. And the man in question was supposed to find his name in the design.

When Shyamita didn't answer right away, Najma asked her again, 'Didi, the name?'

Shyamita looked to see if Geet had heard Najma asking her. But Geet was busy talking to her cousin. So Shyamita quickly whispered to Najma in a low, soft voice, 'Yes, J.'

Jai was exhausted. He had been out all day at the municipal corporation, the bank, and finally at the local community centre his father had been a part of years ago. There had been tons of paperwork to go through. His father's pension, whatever paltry sum he used to get, had been transferred to his mother's name. He had registered an application for renewal of the ration card, and also started the process of turning over the deed of his parents' house to his mother's name. It would all take a long time to be implemented and processed, but he was at peace that he had done everything he had to.

He walked into his mother's room to see her and his sister huddled together and poring through old photo albums. His sister was the first to notice him at the doorway.

'Hey, bro,' she quipped.

His mother looked up from the albums and smiled weakly at him. Clearly she was in pain. He would have to talk to his nut of a sister and tell her not to sound so bloody happy and chirpy. They did lose their father after all. But he also understood what Naina was trying to do. They were both keen on getting their mother to move with Jai to Mumbai. And for that to happen, she had to come out of her grief. Jai realized that it was too soon to expect that from her, but still. The sooner he moved her out of this house, the easier it will be for her to move on and forget the hideous life she had been forced to endure.

'Hey, kid,' he said and shrugging off his jacket walked over to the bed. 'Amma, are you alright?' he asked, his voice ringing with worry and concern. Over the years he had learnt that his mother had a rather nasty habit of bottling up her feelings. She had tried her level best to not let her children get affected by all that she had had to go through.

She smiled at her doting son and said, 'Yes, I'm fine. You must be hungry. Shall we have dinner?'

'What?' Jai jumped off the bed. 'You guys haven't eaten yet? What the hell, Naina?'

Naina, whose eyes sparked fire, said, 'what's wrong with you? We were perusing old albums. So we didn't notice the time.'

'To hell with the albums. Amma doesn't need to relive *all that*,' he rasped, barely containing his anger.

'Are you off your head?' his sister countered him. 'We were looking at *your* school photographs, Jairam Nair. God! You're such a pain.' She had tears streaking down her cheeks now. Quickly wiping them away, she picked an album and threw it at her brother. She scrambled off the bed and ran out of the room.

'Jai, what is the matter with you? Why did you have to shout at Naina?' his mother got on his case too. 'I don't know what I'm going to do with you and your temper,' she slid off the bed, picked up her shawl from the chair next to the door and turned back to her son and said, 'You have to understand one thing, Jai. I am not as weak as you both think I am. I have managed to live my life, however hard it has been and raised two wonderful children. You have to stop living for me now, son. Don't squander away your life just because you have me to take care of. I am not a responsibility. I am your mother. Remember that.' With that, she walked out of the room and disappeared into the kitchen.

Jai just stood there in the middle of his mother's room, clutching the photo album Naina had thrown at him. Was his mother right? Was he not allowing himself to be happy?

He sat down on the edge of the bed and thought of the last conversation he had had with Shyamita. What had she said? *Are you afraid that whatever happened to your parents will happen to us?* Her words were still haunting him. How could he risk everything? How could he risk her happiness? How could he be so selfish and think of only himself? No. He had done the right thing. Yes, he had. But why was he feeling so lost?

His eyes then fell on the photographs that were strewn on the bed. There were photographs of him and Naina when they were children with Amma, and even a few with Appa, probably taken when he was human and sober. Jai opened the album which Naina had thrown at him before her teary exit from the bedroom. They were photographs taken when Amma and Naina had visited him in Mumbai just three months before his 12th board exams. After taking special permission from Principal D'Mello, he and Shyamita had taken Amma and Naina Mumbai-hopping. It had been the best extended weekend of Jai's life.

One particular photograph caught his attention. Shyamita was trying to shove a huge pani puri into her mouth. His little Bengali had always had a thing for pani puri, or 'puchka,' as she would always correct him. They had gone to Chowpatti that evening. And after sitting with his sister on all the baby-rides Shyamita had declared that she was hungry. He still remembered the way he had laughed when the pani puri had burst before it reached Shyamita's mouth and how she had chased him down the beach for having laughed at her antics.

'It's not funny, okay. I'll punch you. Don't laugh at me. Come back here. Okay, I'm tired. Let's go back.' And then when he started walking back towards her, she closed the distance between them and started punching him right there on the beach, in front of everyone. His mother and sister had had quite a laugh at his expense.

Another photograph that caught his attention was one in which Shyamita was sitting with his mother and the two of them were laughing together. Somehow, strangely, he had never seen this photo until today. What had Shyamita said to Amma to make her laugh like that? He had to know.

He got off the bed and walked out of the room, clutching the album.

'Amma,' he called as he entered the kitchen. She was sitting with Naina who looked up when Jai walked in, still teary-eyed. 'Sorry, kid,' he muttered to his sister and gave her a kiss on the top of her head. He then spoke to his mother, 'Amma, where was this photograph taken?' He put the album down on the kitchen table and pointed at the photo in question. 'And what were you two laughing about?'

His mother looked at the photograph and said, 'Oh, what a lovely photo. Shyamu looks so adorable.'

'Yes, yes. She does,' Jai said, exasperated already. 'But where was this taken? And how come I haven't seen it until now?'

'I don't remember where it was taken, Jai,' returned his mother, irritably, but she had a hint of a smile on her face when she said, 'As for you not having seen it until now, I have no answer to that either. But why do you ask? Is it because you want to hear more about Shyamu?'

She turned and looked towards his sister who was now sporting an equally sly smile like their mother.

'Are you two laughing at me?'

'Why? Are you going to chase us down the beach like how Shyamita chased you down?' his sister was quick to respond.

Jai threw his head back and laughed.

'Wow, Shyamu. Your mehndi has darkened so much,' Neetu Aunty exclaimed when Shyamita came down for breakfast the next morning. There were no functions and ceremonies today. This was done so that Geet could be relaxed and well-rested on the day of her wedding, or as her mother had said, 'the bride cannot have dark-circles on her wedding day.'

'Not really, aunty,' Shyamita told her as she poured herself a glass of mango-flavored buttermilk.

'What no?' Neetu Aunty pulled her left hand to examine more closely. 'It is such a beautiful dark maroon,' she smiled. 'Hmmm… this shows how much that Nair boy loves you.'

'Mumma!' Geet yelled from the other end of the dining room. 'Mumma, could you please come here?'

As Neetu Aunty made her way to her daughter, Shyamita caught Geet's eye and mouthed a *thank you* to her.

So her mehndi was a dark shade of maroon. It was believed that if a girl's mehndi was dark, then it meant that her beloved really loved her.

Jai loved her? Hah! What a joke! If he did, he would have been here with her. But no. He was god knows where. Probably out at some book-launch or book-signing, she said to herself. She promised herself that she would be happy and cheerful all day and not think of Jai at all.

Shyamita noticed that a table was laden with all sorts of Punjabi chaat and delicacies. She generously loaded her plate with everything that was on the table, and in a small bowl, she placed a deliciously fat pani puri. After placing the bowl in her plate, she sat down on a chair and began to devour her breakfast. She was just about to shove the huge pani puri into her mouth when Raman kaka ushered 'that Nair boy' in.

And as expected, the pani-puri broke in Shyamita's hand, splattering her white kurta with its contents.

20

Jai watched as Shyamita's face turned pink and then crimson. Twelve years on, and she still hadn't learned how to eat pani puri. She pushed her plate away and got up from her chair. For a second Jai thought she was going to come to him. But then she turned and climbed up the stairs and disappeared.

Jai quickly scanned the room for Geet and spotted her standing with her cousins. But she was hardly listening to them. She was too busy glowering at him. He shrugged and before Geet could excuse herself from her cousins, streaked across the dining room, took the stairs three at a time and reached Shyamita's door.

It stood slightly ajar, so Jai knocked twice and pushed it open. She was sitting on the bed, head bent down and her shoulders shaking. She was crying. He knew. And it was entirely his fault.

Stepping into the room, he closed the door behind him. At the sound it made, Shyamita jerked her head up. She looked so beautiful in the morning light streaking from the open windows. Dressed in a white kurta, which now had splotches of the water from the pani puri, and a pink patiala, her hair left loose around her shoulders, her cheeks red from the crying, and her big brown eyes swimming in tears. Jai felt like the biggest jerk on the planet. How could he have done this to her?

'What...what are you doing here?' she mumbled, amidst tears.

Jai walked towards her and knelt down in front of her. Her hands were knotted together in her lap and he could see her digging her nails into her skin. He put his hands on hers and squeezed tightly. She didn't look up at him again. She just sat there, staring at their hands entwined. A soft sob escaping every now and then. Jai didn't say anything either.

Finally, he laid his head in her lap. Shyamita immediately pulled out her hands from underneath him and placed them on either side of her. For the longest time, Jai thought she would just sit like that and not say or do anything. But just when he was about to give up hope, she threaded her fingers into his hair. He sagged with relief against her legs and wrapped his arms around her waist, the top of his head now touching her belly. She ran her fingers through his hair and gently massaged his scalp.

'Why did you leave me, Jai?' Shyamita's voice shook with emotion, as tears clogged at the back of her throat.

Jai looked up at her then. The red in her cheeks had reduced considerably, and it was now a soft shade of pink. Tears still glistened in her eyes, but at least they were not threatening to overflow. However, it was her mouth that made him forget what he had come here to tell her. Her lips, pink and lush, were quivering. He wanted nothing more than to bite that lower lip and taste her sweetness.

But he couldn't do that. Not yet. First, he had to tell her everything. She needed to know. She deserved to know.

He cleared his throat, tightened his grip around her waist and said in a voice that he hoped was calm and comforting, 'Mithi, I never left you.'

'You did,' she cut in before he could speak further. 'You left me, just like the last time,' and a solitary tear slid down her cheek.

He gently wiped the tear away with his thumb. 'I'm sorry, sweetheart. I'm sorry for being a moron.'

'You didn't need to be one, you know,' she added. But she still wasn't looking at him.

So Jai cupped her face in his hands and forced her to look into his eyes. 'I know, baby. Sorry,' he said tenderly.

Shyamita looked into Jai's eyes and what she saw in those chocolate brown depths sent a warm rush through her body. Her heart wanted to leap out of her chest and tell him just how much she loved him. But she was scared. She wanted him to open up. She wanted him to tell her why he left her.

'I thought I was doing the right thing by you, Mithi. I didn't want to drag you into something that you would come to regret eventually,' he added.

'How do you know what is right for me and what is not? And what am I going to regret? You didn't call or text me even, Jai,' she accused. 'And then when Geet and Karan told me that you're not going to be here for the remaining ceremonies I thought...I really thought...,' she broke on a sob.

'Thought what, Mithi?' he asked her. 'What did you think?'

'That you don't want to see me anymore. That may be, you hate me' she said softly.

'Shyamita Bose!' He stood up. 'How can you be so silly? How can you even think that? Why on earth would I hate you?' Jai stared at her in utter disbelief.

'It's not difficult to come to that conclusion, Jairam Nair,' she replied, her voice shaking again. 'You don't share anything with me. You're happy with the way things are. You don't want to work towards making this...us...work,' she added.

He caught her by the shoulders and hauled her to her feet. The action caught Shyamita off-guard and she looked up at him with eyes as wide as saucers.

'Let's just get one thing straight, Mithi. I can never hate you. Are you kidding me?' He let go of her shoulders and ran his fingers through his hair. 'How on earth did that thought even enter your mind? How can I hate you when I...,' he broke off just as he caught sight of a book on her nightstand.

Frowning, he walked over to the table and picked up the book. Slowly, very slowly, he turned back to face Shyamita. 'Where did you get this?' he asked in a low voice, holding up the copy of his book, his face hard in the sunlight.

Jai's question was met with about ten seconds of silence. And in that time, he could feel his temper rising. If she had read the letters she would know what his life had been. Granted he had come here with the intention of telling her. But this was no way for her to find out. He wanted to be the one to tell her.

'Where did you get this book, Shyamita?' he asked her again. This time, Jai's voice was harder.

'I...uhh...I found it on your bookshelf,' she said, in a small voice, her head bent. She was staring at her toes which were painted a metallic pink.

'And how did it find its way here?' Jai went on.

I...uhh...Jai...I...,' she mumbled. 'I must have packed it with my things that morning when we were in a hurry to leave,' she said and looking up at him, she added, 'I'm sorry, Jai. I never meant to take it.'

But Jai wasn't even listening to what she was saying. 'Did you read it?' he asked her.

Jai...I...,' she began.

'Just say yes or no, Shyamita,' he cut her short.

'Yes, I did.'

He didn't say anything. But he was watching her carefully, as though he was trying to read her.

'Jai, it doesn't matter. You grew out of that, didn't you? Lalita Aunty is happy now because you're happy,' she told him in a calm and placating voice.

'You think I've grown out of it?' he asked in a low voice that sent an eerie shiver down Shyamita's spine.

'You think I will ever get over the sound of my mother crying in agony and pain as her husband beat her and broke her will? You really think that?'

Shyamita closed the distance between them and placed her hand on his cheek. 'Jai…I didn't mean it like that,' she began but only to be cut short by him again.

'I don't need your pity,' and saying that he slapped her hand away. 'I don't need you to feel sorry for me or my mother.' He moved away from her towards the window. 'This is why I never told you any of this in all the years that I've known you. I knew you'd pity me. I knew you'd never understand. I don't need your pity, do you get that?'

Tears stung at the back of Shyamita's throat. How could someone be so blind and misguided? But she was not going to defend herself. She was done defending herself. She was done trying to make him see her point. She took a breath, steadied her nerves, and said, 'I *get* that, Jai. I'm sorry for having read the book without your permission. Had I known this is how you would react, I would never have read it. I know you don't believe me when I say that I did not deliberately pack it with my things, but that doesn't matter anymore. I cannot help you if you don't want to help yourself.'

'Please leave me alone, Jai. I fell weak the last time you left me. But I assure you, this time I won't.' She was proud that her voice did not shake while she said this. She turned away from him then and walked towards the door. Upon reaching there, she turned back and said, 'Goodbye, Jairam Nair,' and walked out of the room.

'I am so goddamn proud of you, Shyamu,' Geet was giddy with happiness when a little while later Shyamita told her what had transpired between her and Jai. 'Serves him right. What'd he think? He could just waltz in here whenever he felt like it? So what if you read his book? Sooner or later he would have had to tell you. And why is he so upset about you reading his book anyway? Thousands must have read it.'

'No. He never got around to publishing it, Geet. It's just a collection of letters and poems he'd written while growing up. I don't think he intends to ever publish them,' Shyamita informed her. She felt horrible for having read the letters. But she had had no idea Jai would react the way he did. She didn't know where he was right at this moment. She had walked out of the room and gone straight out to the garden to find her bearings once again. It was she who had ended things this time. She wouldn't grieve, she told herself.

'Okay. He didn't want to publish them. But what's the big deal about you reading them?' Geet was just not able to wrap her head around the way Jai had reacted.

'I read it without his knowledge, Geet. And that was wrong of me,' Shyamita had to remind her.

'God! This propriety and all is beyond me,' Geet said in an irritated voice. 'Anyway, let it be, Shyamu. I'll find you a nice, good-looking Punjabi boy. Okay?' she teased.

Shyamita smiled, and hugged her friend tightly. Geet hugged her back, equally tightly. They sat there on the garden bench, remembering their school days. They laughed and cried and then laughed some more.

Tomorrow was the wedding. She didn't know when she would meet Geet again. She wasn't sure when she would come back to India again. She would probably ask Ma and Baba to come and visit her in Paris. Shaunak was moving to Marseilles by the end of the year. The company he worked for was sending him on a project for three years. Coming to India would be too painful for her now.

As if, somehow sensing her train of thought, Geet put her arm over Shyamita's shoulder and said, 'Karan and I will come and see you in Paris, Shyamu. He can go visit the catacombs all day. You and I can sit in a café and just be us. Okay?'

Shyamita smiled sadly at how easily Geet was able to read her. But Jai, after so many years of knowing her, had still not been able to realize that she could never pity him.

She wanted to be the one who would pull him out of the whole thing. She knew she could do it. But Jai just didn't see it that way. He was too pigheaded.

Sighing inwardly, she realized she had just one more day to get through. She would leave for Pune in the morning, day after tomorrow. Away from Mumbai. Away from Jai.

Just then, Raman kaka walked up to them with a large pink envelope in his hand. Handing it over to Geet, he said, 'Bibiji, Karan baba left this for you.'

Geet jumped up and excitedly scanned the garden for a glimpse of her fiancé. Shyamita felt a stab of jealousy, but she quickly ignored it and said, 'He can't see you, Geet. That's not allowed.' She pulled Geet back down on to the bench.

Geet slumped back in her seat and pouted petulantly. 'I hate these stupid customs,' she muttered.

'Just hang in there, love. You'll see him tomorrow,' Shyamita consoled her.

At that, Geet's eyes lit up like Diwali. Fervently nodding her head, she glanced at the envelope. Within seconds, she had ripped open the seal and pulled out a large Archies' card: white, pink with loads of glitter and hearts. It was so Geet. Shyamita saw her friend's eyes brim with tears as she opened the card and read the words out loud –

Just a few hours more, baby.

Geet sighed, closed the card and crushed it to her chest. She smiled, lovestruck. She and Karan had always been like this. Even when they were in school, Karan would buy her flowers and chocolates. Jai would tease his friend mercilessly and Shyamita would try hard to not let her jealousy show on her face.

Even thinking about those times, about Jai, made her heart weep.

Goodbye, Jairam Nair.

Jai was miserable. What the hell had just happened? He had gone over to apologize to Shyamita, to make amends with her. But instead, he'd acted like a total jerk again. And he'd hurt her again. There used to be a time when he would have punched the living daylights out of the person who tried to hurt Shyamita. But today, he was the one doing all the hurting. How had he become like this?

After half an hour of silent brooding, Jai decided that it was all for the best. She would go back to Paris and he would go back to living a life...without her. The last two words hurt. He couldn't imagine a life without her. Granted they had been apart for nearly twelve years, but now that they had found each other again, was it going to be easy to let go?

Another half an hour later, Jai thought he was losing his head. He picked up his cell phone and dialed.

Shyamita answered after three rings. 'Hello?' she muttered groggily into the phone. 'Whoever this is, you better have a good reason for calling at this hour.'

Jai had to smile at that.

'I do have a good reason for calling, Mithi,' he said and he heard her breath hitch.

'Jai?'

'Yes.'

'Are you okay? Is everything okay? Aunty? Naina?' she asked, frantic with worry.

'Yes. Everything is okay. Mom and Naina are in Bangalore,' he told her.

Shyamita absorbed this new information before asking him, 'What are they doing Bangalore, Jai?' She spoke so sweetly and softly to him that had she been in front of him right then, he would have kissed her senseless.

'Appa died a couple of days ago,' he said solemnly.

'Oh, no,' came her reply. Then a few seconds of silence later, 'I'm so sorry, Jai. Is that where you were the last couple of days? Is that why you didn't call or text me?' Shyamita had to know.

'Yes,' was all he said. 'Mithi?'

'Hmmm?'

'I...uhh...nothing. Goodnight.'

And he disconnected.

21

Shyamita spent the remainder of the night tossing and turning restlessly. At the crack of dawn, unable to sleep, she got out of bed. Furiously brushing her teeth, she scrubbed her face and pulled her hair back into a high ponytail and walked downstairs. A lot of the elders were already up and about, getting ready for the big day. She knew Geet would be asleep upstairs but she didn't want to disturb her. The bride needed all the rest she could get. So Shyamita decided to step out for a short walk.

Mumbai was already bustling with traffic. The familiar sights and sounds of the city engulfed her and for a while she felt secure and safe. But then, the events of the last one week caught up with her. It was Jai's phone call from last night which had her most worried. Stopping for chai outside a roadside tea-stall, she went over whatever little conversation she and Jai had had over the phone.

Shyamita had wanted to comfort him, but before she could say anything he had cut the line. She went through the conversation again in her head and remembered that there was something he was going to say in the end. What had he been trying to say? It was very unlike Jai to leave things hanging. She saw a tiny glimmer of hope but squashed it immediately. She had to move on.

By the time she got back home, Geet was awake and on the verge of a panic attack.

'Shyamuuu!' she shrieked as soon as she saw Shyamita. 'I've been looking everywhere for you. I was just about to call Jai and ask him if he had come here last night and you'd gone with him.'

'I'd just gone for a walk,' Shyamita told her in a way that said she had been overreacting.

'Oh, alright. Sorry. Blame it on the pre-wedding nerves, okay?' she looked at Shyamita apologetically.

Shyamita laughed at that. 'Let's get you ready, missy.'

And Geet squealed excitedly.

'Jairam Nair, you listen to me loud and clear,' his sister bellowed at him on the phone. 'I don't care what nonsense you've got in that stupid head of yours, but you better go and make things right with Shyamita.'

'Naina, will you let me get a word in?' he asked but she shot him down again.

'No. Shut up. I've had enough of your stupid boorish ways.'

'I am being a boor? Really?' he started but…

'Shut up! Don't interrupt me. Wait a minute…what… oh, wait. Amma wants to talk to you,' he could hear her saying to their mother – *don't let him off lightly*.

'Jai?' his mother spoke.

'Hi, Amma.'

'What is this I'm hearing? Geet told Naina that you spoke very rudely to Shyamita.' Apparently they were past the niceties now and he was being treated like a boy who'd been caught stealing sweets.

'Amma, I…,' he began, but it seemed his mother was determined to cut him short just like his sister.

'I don't want to hear anything, Jai. I know how much you love that girl. You two were inseparable in school and then you both behaved stupidly and spoiled things for yourselves. But now, you are getting a second chance. And you will not mess it up. Am I clear?' Although his mother was in another city, Jai still looked a little abashed for being admonished by his mother. For god's sake, he was thirty years old. But that didn't stop his mother from talking to him as if he was still a schoolboy.

'Am I clear, Jai?' she asked again.

'Yes, Amma,' he said softly.

'She did not do anything wrong, Jai,' his mother went on. 'So what if she read your book? You were going to tell her anyway. Didn't she, in a way, make it easy for you? You didn't have to go through the ordeal of telling her.'

'Yes, Amma, you're right. I didn't think of it that way,' he confessed and at just about the same time he realized what a big moron he'd been, again.

They spoke for just a while longer after that with Naina telling him he should tell Shyamita how much he loved her by taking her out to the Taj for dinner. He thanked his sister for her words of wisdom and hung up.

He walked into his closet and stood in front of the mirror. *Was he really in love?* His reflection laughed at him for asking a question that had such a ridiculously obvious answer.

'Amma...that was some terrific acting,' Naina gave her mother a tight hug as soon as they had finished speaking to Jai. 'You didn't even let him speak. Wow. Now I know where I get that from.'

Lalita Nair smiled at her daughter indulgently. Today was a happy day for them. They had finally managed to make Jai realize the depth of his feelings for Shyamita.

'Your brother has been in love with Shyamita probably from the first day they met in school,' she told Naina. 'When he would come home for the holidays, he would only talk about her. I used to think the boy had no other friends.'

Naina laughed at that. It seemed everything would fall into place now. They would all be happy again. *If only Jai wasn't too late already,* she thought but didn't voice it out loud to her mother.

The hotel where the wedding was being held had been decked with thousands of yellow and white gerberas and jacarandas. The entrance to the wedding hall had a beautiful water fountain with pink lotuses. The wedding hall was a mesmerizing kaleidoscope of gold, red, pink, and white. There were flowers and tiny bells everywhere, the floor along the walls were lined with small oil lamps. Wedding guests were given a bag of chocolates, a silver coin and one disposable camera each. This had been Karan's idea. He didn't want just the professional photographers to give them a typical wedding album.

When Shyamita saw Jai dancing in the baraat, she all but had a meltdown. *How could he be so normal? How could he pretend everything was okay?* When the baraat stopped at the entrance to the hotel, Neetu Aunty greeted her future son-in-law in typical Punjabi style. Shyamita caught sight of Jai who was standing behind Karan, smiling. When their eyes met, he winked at her and smiled his thousand-watt smile, sending Shyamita's heart into overdrive.

The wedding ceremony was beautiful. Geet and Karan had insisted on having the wedding during the day. In

Geet's words, she wanted to drive into the sunset with her husband. She looked like the million-dollar bride she was and Karan looked very much in love with his bride, as he had always been. Shyamita had been right next to Geet during all the ceremonies and Jai stood next to Karan. She tried her level best to not be affected by his presence. Every now and then he would flash a smile at her and Shyamita's brain would turn into chocolate pudding.

The saat-phere, during which the bride and groom took seven rounds around the holy fire which had been lit amidst various Vedic chants and mantras, is the most important feature of a traditional Indian wedding. And as Shyamita watched Geet and Karan take their ceremonial rounds around the fire, she couldn't help but feel a certain melancholy. She would have loved for this to be her wedding to the man of her dreams – who was right at that moment, talking animatedly to Neetu Aunty. She wanted to be a bride. She wanted to be Jai's bride.

Shyamita realized she had to get away. This was all becoming too much for her to take. But she had to pull herself together. Falling apart now was not an option. She had made certain decisions last night and she was going to stick to them. She couldn't wait for the vidaai. She had to get away from here. From Jai.

'What? You're leaving now?' Geet shrieked. 'But isn't your train for Pune tomorrow morning, Shyamu?'

'It was, Geet. But I need to go. I can't be around Jai any longer and pretend everything is okay,' Shyamita told her, her voice shaking. Jai had been behaving very strangely all throughout the wedding ceremony. He spoke to everyone and even danced with a few of Geet's cousins and her mother. He was back to being normal. And she couldn't be around him and not get affected. Tears once again clogged the back of her throat, but she furiously blinked them back. She was not going to fall weak again, she vowed.

'But, Shyamu...,' Geet started crying. Tears streaked down her cheeks, threatening to ruin her perfect make-up. Shyamita quickly pulled out tissues and dabbed Geet's face gently so as to not spoil her makeup.

'Shh...it's okay, Geet,' she told her softly. 'You and Karan can come and visit me whenever you want, okay?'

Geet nodded silently, tears still flowing down her cheeks. 'Geet, if you don't stop crying, you'll ruin your make-up,' Shyamita told her in an effort to stop her from crying.

But somehow that made Geet cry even harder. 'Who cares about the stupid make-up?' she wailed.

Shyamita smiled at her friend and hugged her tightly. 'I love you, Geet Chadda. And I'm going to miss you.' And then the tears she had held onto for the whole day just poured right out of her.

Jai scanned the gathered crowd for Shyamita, but couldn't spot her. It was time for the vidaai. Almost all the women who were gathered at the exit of the hotel were teary-eyed. Aunties and cousins were constantly dabbing at the corner of their eyes with tissues and handkerchiefs. But Shyamita was nowhere to be seen.

'Geet, where is she?' Jai asked Geet just before she got into Karan's decked up BMW 7 series.

Geet looked like she was about to kill him. She took a deep, calming breath and said, 'I am not going to tell you. Leave her alone,' and turned to get into the car.

But Jai was quick. He caught her arm and turned her to face him, which turned out to be a big mistake because Geet Chadda did the one thing she had been dying to do all week. She punched Jai in the nose. Beside her, Karan struggled hard to stifle his laughter. The rest of the family and wedding guests just looked on at the incredulous scene these three presented.

'Now you want to know where she is?' Geet reached supersonic levels. Bridezilla was back. 'She's gone, Jai. She's on her way to Pune by the five-thirty train. And thank god she's going. Shyamu doesn't need a jackass like you. She's been doing nothing but crying these past few days. Do you have any idea how much she loves you? I hope you rot in hell. Go write another bestseller or whatever. But leave Shyamu alone,' she ended her tirade because she had to stop for air.

With blood dripping from his nose and staining the front of his cream kurta, Jai stared at Geet, incredulously. He'd just been punched by this diminutive figure. But she'd also told him the very thing he wanted to hear. He glanced at his watch and saw that he still had twenty minutes before Shyamita's train left. It shouldn't take him that long to get to CST.

He kissed Geet on her forehead, hugged Karan carefully, so as to not let the blood still pouring out of his nose stain his clothes, then sprinted to his Volvo.

But ten minutes later, Jai was ready to curse Mumbai's traffic to the deepest recesses of hell. He was stuck in a terrible jam, just five minutes away from CST. Looking around frantically for a gap in the rows of cars so that he could wheedle out his monstrous Volvo, Jai cursed the day he had bought the SUV.

There was nothing to it. He would have to leave his car and make a run for it.

So he quickly got out, locked his car and was just about to start off when the shrill sound of a whistle almost deafened him. He turned around to scream at the bloody idiot, but to his amazement it was the same hawaldar with his henna-colored moustache he and Shyamita had met at Marine

Drive. Jai was sure the man had been sent to navigate and clear up the traffic. He smiled at the man and was about to turn around when the hawaldar said, 'Hello, sirjee. Is everything okay?' He looked at Jai from top to bottom, taking in his broken nose and bloodstained kurta.

Jai had to stop. 'Hello, hello,' he said in a hurry.

'Where is madamjee? And what happened to your nose, sirjee?' the man was clearly in the mood for chit-chat.

Suddenly, inspiration struck, and he blurted, 'She is leaving me, hawaldar sahib. We had a fight and now she is going to catch the train to Pune from CST. I need to get there, but...,' with his hand he gestured towards the maddening traffic.

Fortunately, the hawaldar seemed to understand Jai's predicament and said, 'Arre, sirjee, not to worry. I will drop you. I like this madamjee. Did she break your nose?' He chuckled as Jai climbed onto the pillion seat of his motorcycle.

Jai reached the railway station with just one minute to spare. He thanked the hawaldar from the bottom of his heart and promised to meet him for chai one evening when all was well between him and 'madamjee'.

Shyamita's train was on platform number two. He had no idea what her seat number was and he didn't have the time to check her name on the lists that were pasted outside every coach. Just as the wheels started turning, Jai got into a coach and began his search. Some of the passengers were stunned to see him in his bloodstained clothes, probably thinking he was a serial killer on the loose.

The train began to gain speed as it left the platform and Jai knew he had no other choice but to pull the chain. But just as he was about to, an ice-cream vendor passed down the aisle. He quickly put a hand on the vendor's shoulder to stop him. The vendor taking in Jai's bloody nose and clothes almost had a heart attack before handing him two cups of vanilla ice-cream. Pocketing the money, the poor guy practically ran out of the compartment.

Shaking his head, Jai went over to a booth where there were three couples sitting. Apologizing for interrupting the conversation and stepping on one man's shoes, Jai reached up and pulled the chain. He turned back to watch the three couples scuttle out of their seats and disappear into another compartment. About ten seconds later, the ticket-master appeared. Jai smiled. It was time for some action.

As the train lurched to a stop, the other passengers around Shyamita began peering out of the window. Somebody ran into their compartment, panting while saying frantically, 'there is some mad man on the train. He has blood all over his clothes.'

The chaos and panic that ensued after such a statement was quite understandable. Many people disembarked the train immediately, as the train was not too far from the station. An old man, before jumping off the train said to her, 'What are you waiting for? You want that mad man to kill you?'

Quickly wiping her tears, Shyamita stood up and heaved her bag out from underneath the seat. But no sooner had she taken one step forward, than the door to the compartment burst open and in walked the ticket-master and behind him stood Jai. There was dried blood near his nose and his kurta was stained with blood too. His hands were cuffed and he held two cups of vanilla ice-cream in them. And right behind Jai, stood two police constables.

Grinning, Jai said to her, 'I've got to say whatever I have to, quickly. Because this guy here,' he jerked his head sideways towards the ticket-master, 'plans to throw me into the railway jail.'

Shyamita would have laughed had she not been worried about all the blood. 'Jai, what happ...,' but he stopped her before she could complete her query.

'Hear me out, Mithi. Please?'

She nodded, and he smiled before saying, 'I've been a real moron. I've been complete and total jerk. I've been horrible and nasty and rude and...,' but Shyamita cut in. 'Jai, I know all that.'

He smiled, his eyes twinkled, and Shyamita's heart began beating faster than a bullet train.

'Okay, okay...so...umm...jeez, isn't it hot in here? Couldn't you have booked a seat in the AC coach?' he asked.

'Jairam Nair!' Shyamita almost screamed. There were people gathering around to get a good look at the 'mad' man.

'Yeah, okay. Sir,' he addressed one of the constables, 'do you mind taking off my handcuffs for just a minute?' The constable who had already sensed what this was all about, reached into his pocket and pulled out a small key. He inserted it into the slot on the handcuffs and unlocked it. 'Thank you,' Jai smiled at the man before taking two steps forward. He placed the ice-cream cups on the blue berth next to him and finally looked at Shyamita properly.

'Have you been crying?' he asked her.

'Jai, is that really what you came here to ask me?' she was getting impatient now.

'Well, no. I guess I'd better get on with it then, right?'

'You think?'

Jai got down on one knee, right there in the middle of the dirty compartment and said,

'Mithi, the last time you and I were on a train, we walked away empty-handed. But this time, I promise there will be no pain, As this is what *we* have always wanted. Because I know you love me, Shyamita Bose, Just as much as I love you. Because of you, I let that bulldozer, Geet, punch me in the nose And for that reason (among many others), I want to marry you.'

Applause rang throughout the compartment. Some people whistled. The ticket-master and the two constables shook their heads.

But Jai was waiting for an answer. 'Mithi?'

After staring at him for a few seconds, Shyamita asked, 'Did Geet really punch you?'

'Clearly it is absolutely essential that you know the details of *that* now,' Jai muttered, exasperated.

Shyamita laughed. 'Jairam Nair, I've been in love with you all my life. The last time we were on a train, we both behaved stupidly and decided that it would be best to just be friends. I will always remember that stupid Aisha…'

'Mithi, I never loved that girl. God! You're still stuck on that.'

'Yes, well, you're the one who said you loved her. You broke my heart that day, Jai,' she ended on a soft sob.

Jai took Shyamita's hands in his and said, 'Mithi, I was never in love with Aisha. I said that only because your question that day threw me off-guard. Do you know what Ms. Jacinta told me that evening after our paper?'

Shyamita shook her head. And Jai went on, 'She told me in her own way that I should never let you go. And today, I've realized that a teacher is always right. I don't intend to let you go again, Shyamita Bose,' he ended emphatically.

Shyamita stared incredulously at Jai. 'She…she actually said that?'

This time it was Jai who nodded.

Shyamita smiled and bent her head forward to rest it against his. 'Jai,' she said softly, 'I'm glad you finally realized the truth in Ms Jacinta's words. Because there is nothing more I want in this world than to have you in my life. You are my world, Jai. I love you'

Jai smiled and rose from his position on the floor. He picked up the two cups of ice-cream from the berth, and handing one to Shyamita he said, 'This is probably the first time a couple has exchanged cups of vanilla ice-cream instead of engagement rings.'

Shyamita and Jai did actually exchange engagement rings two months later. Jai had wanted the engagement to take place sooner, but Shyamita insisted on waiting for Geet and Karan to return from their honeymoon in Spain and Italy, which in hindsight, Jai realized, was a good thing. He didn't want his engagement photos to show him sporting a bandage on his nose.

A month after their engagement, they were married on Marine Drive. It was a simple ceremony with just family and their closest friends. But the guest of honor was Hawaldar Kale, the man who would always be Jai's hero and savior for having helped him get to the train station in time.

On their way home, after the wedding ceremony, Shyamita hugged her husband tightly as she sat behind him on his KTM. She was in a sari again, but this time she had no qualms holding onto Jai. As soon as they reached home, she ran into their bedroom, leaving Jai standing at the doorway.

'What is it, Mithi?' he called after her, worried.

'Wait right there, Jai,' came her response.

Within moments she was back. 'Mithi, what the…,' his voice trailed when she stopped right in front of him with a wide grin on her face.

'Jai,' Shyamita said, her voice low and soft, 'this is for you.' She placed a small envelope in his hand. It was old and slightly worn off at the corners.

'What is this, Mithi?' he asked her, curious.

'Open it,' she instructed.

Jai carefully opened the envelope and pulled out a small white and blue card. A basket of flowers adorned the front of the card, with the words *To My Love* etched above it.

'Mithi…,' he said, but Shyamita shook her head. 'Open the card, Jai,' she said.

He did.

Shyamita watched the emotions play out on Jai's face as he read the card she had picked out for him twelve years ago. Within a matter of seconds, she was enveloped into a bone-crushing hug.

'Idiot girl,' he said, before he ravaged her mouth.

Epilogue

Seven years, five more bestsellers, sixteen paintings and three daughters later, Jai and Shyamita were living happily at their home on Carter Road. Jai's mother shuffled between Mumbai and Paris, which was where Naina was working. They visited Shyamita's mother in Pune almost every alternate weekend. After Shyamita's father passed away five years ago, her mother found it increasingly difficult to make the journey from Pune to Mumbai by herself. Shyamita's brother Shaunak was working in Barcelona at an automobile company and, Jai suspected, dating a Spanish girl.

Today, Jai and Shyamita were celebrating their seventh wedding anniversary and their home had been turned into a madhouse. There were five children (their three daughters, and Geet and Karan's twin boys) running around and causing mayhem. 'Geet, will you please tell your son not to lift up my daughter's skirt?' Jai bellowed at Geet.

'Shut up, Jai. Or I'll punch you on your nose again,' she said and Jai grinned.

By evening, the house was packed with friends and family. The children were with one of Shyamita's cousins who had gladly taken on the role of babysitter for the evening.

After making sure everyone had a flute of champagne in their hand, Jai cleared his throat before saying, 'If you could just stop your chit-chat for a few minutes and pay attention to this very handsome man who's about to say something awesome, I'd really appreciate it.'

'Jai!' Shyamita walked up to him and muttered under her breath, 'what are you doing?'

But Jai shushed her. 'You're going to want to hear this,' he told her.

Then he turned to his audience and began.

'Thank you all for coming here this evening and being a part of our special day. Each and every one of you has been instrumental in getting us together and keeping us together, too. So, really, thank you.'

'And now,' he said and turned to face Shyamita, 'to my wife, I'd just like to say… Mithi, thank you for being the only one who managed to steal my heart so many years ago. Thank you for not returning it to me even though I may have given you countless reasons to do so over the years. Thank you for the wonderful family you've given me and for the lovely home you've given us all. Thank you for…well, I think I'm out of words.' He took a deep breath and went on, 'All I can say now is that I love you.' After a moment's pause he said, 'Anyway, they are the only words that matter.'

Acknowledgements:

I have a lot of people to thank and honestly do not know how to go about it. There are a lot of people who have helped me achieve whatever I have today. But still, I will try.

Accha, for being the first and most wonderful man in my life.

Amma, for giving me the courage to live every dream.

Nikita, for being my guardian angel, my first reader, my official stylist…and the best sister.

Appu Ettan, for believing in me, even when I didn't believe in myself.

Prachir, for always standing by me.

Fizza, for being my first critic, and my soul sister.

Mama, Raji Velliamma, Ammamma, Babymema, Sunil Velliacchan, for always looking out for me.

Abhishek, Anand, Ammu Chechi, Malu, Madhavi and Vikram, for being a part of some of my best childhood memories.

Das Uncle, for all those early morning dreams you had of me. They're finally coming true, Das Uncle! ☺

Mrs Rao, my favourite English teacher, for being the voice in my head even twelve years after school.

My awesome editor, *Arushi,* for helping me perfect Jai and Shyamita's story.

My publisher, Amrita, for being my fairy godmother.

Reet Singh, Aarti Venkatraman, and *Adite Banerjie*, fellow writers (I am so psyched I can actually say that now!) for being such a fabulous support system.

All my students, for being bursts of sunshine, or showers of rain, on my most miserable days. I love you all.

…and finally, *RB*, for being the 'extra' to my ordinary. And for bringing me to the light.

– This book is dedicated to you all.